# The Book of Fairy Princes

For LOIS, LAURENCE, MARK, and SYLVIA,
and for all other boys and girls
who have had nine candles
on their birthday cake.

Isabel Wyatt

# The Book of
# Fairy Princes

Floris Books

Illustrations by Natasha Stewart

First published by A Dakers, London in 1949
This edition published in 1994 by Floris Books

British Library CIP Data available

ISBN 0-86315-528-6

Printed in Great Britain
by BPC Wheatons, Exeter

# Contents

# Contents

# The Princess in the Ivory Tower

The King and Queen of Golden Land once had a little daughter. She had long, shining, golden hair, and she was full of joy and laughter, for none is ever sad in Golden Land. There the sun never ceases its gentle shining, and there are no storms or tempests; flowers bloom all the year round, and there is always ripe fruit on the trees. Everyone there is kind; everyone is happy; and everyone is so rich that the city of the King is built of jewels and the streets are paved with gold.

When the little Princess was seven years old, the Queen cut off her golden hair and laid it carefully away.

"Why do you cut off my hair, Mother?" asked the little Princess.

"So that you may grow some more," replied the Queen.

And the King and the Queen called the nurse of the little Princess to them, and said to her:

"It is time for the little Princess to leave Golden Land and go dwell in the Great Forest."

Now the Princess's nurse was a fairy; so that night, while the Princess was sleeping, she laid her on a cloud as white and soft as swansdown and floated away with her.

When dawn came, they were very far from Golden Land, moving gently over the tops of trees — so many trees that they looked from above like the green billows of an endless ocean. This was the Great Forest. At last they floated over a clearing in the forest, and in the clearing was a tall tower built all of ivory. And the Fairy Nurse took the sleeping Princess from the swansdown cloud and laid her on an ivory bed in the ivory tower.

When the Princess woke up in the morning she looked about her, and everything was strange.

"Where am I, Nurse?" she asked.

"You are in the Great Forest," replied the Fairy Nurse.

"Isn't this my father's golden palace?" asked the Princess.

"No. It is your own ivory tower," replied the Fairy Nurse.

"When shall I go back to Golden Land?" asked the Princess.

"When your hair has grown again," replied the Fairy Nurse.

The Princess looked at her hair, which hung round her face, cut quite short, like a page-boy's.

"But, Nurse, it Isn't growing at all yet!" she said.

"No," said the Fairy Nurse. "It won't grow till you learn to spin."

"When can I learn to spin, Nurse?" asked the Princess.

"When you are fourteen years old," replied the Fairy Nurse.

At first the little Princess longed to go back to Golden Land, and felt very sad whenever she remembered the King and Queen. After the golden daylight in her father's city, the Great Forest seemed very dark and gloomy; and after the warmth and brightness of her father's palace, the ivory tower seemed bleak and cold. In Golden Land no flowers have any thorns, and in the Great Forest she used at first to cry when she pricked herself on the briars from which she was gathering wild roses. Also, in Golden Land she had never seen black clouds or hail or thunderstorms or bitter weather, and at first these frightened her.

But in time she grew not to mind the thorns because the roses were so beautiful, and not to mind black clouds and hail and thunderstorms and bitter weather because after the rain the earth smelt so sweet. After the hardships of winter came the loveliness of spring.

In the Great Forest the trees and the flowers and the fruits and the grasses and the birds and the bees and the butterflies were quite different from those she had known in Golden Land, and soon she began to be interested in watching them and playing with them and learning all about them. Presently she ceased to find the Great Forest dark and gloomy, ceased to find the ivory tower bleak and cold. And the time came when she actually really liked living in a forest, in a tower which was all her own!

Then the little Princess began to go into all the rooms in the ivory tower, and she found them filled with absorbing and exciting things which she had never seen before. There was only one door which was always locked, and through this she had never been. She often pressed on the thumb-latch, but never would it open.

"What is beyond the locked door, Nurse?" she asked.

"You will find out when you open it," replied the Fairy Nurse.

"When will that be, Nurse?" asked the little Princess.

"When the right time comes," replied the Fairy Nurse.

"When will the right time come, Nurse?" asked the little Princess.

"When you are fourteen years old," replied the Fairy Nurse.

So the Princess had to go on waiting to know what was beyond the locked door.

But at last her fourteenth birthday came; and the moment she woke up in the morning, she went to the door and pressed again on the thumb-latch; and this time it was not locked, but opened at her touch.

She looked inside very eagerly, and she saw that it led to a narrow staircase, which curled up and up and up inside the ivory tower. She climbed and climbed and climbed, until the stairs came to an end outside another narrow door. She pressed on the latch and it opened, and she stepped forward into a little room, quite empty except for a stool and a spinning-wheel.

It was a round room, right at the top of the ivory tower; and it had twelve windows, so that on every side the Princess could see the sunlight and the clouds, the insects flitting by, the birds busy with their nests, the leaf-buds swelling, the pollen drifting, the wind moving in the treetops. She had never been able to watch all these things so closely and clearly before.

And at night the stars seemed so near that she felt she could reach up and touch them.

She found the little round room at the top of the tower so delightful that she asked her Fairy Nurse if she might live in it for always.

And the Fairy Nurse replied:

"You may live in the little round room until your hair touches the ground."

Then the Princess opened wide all the twelve windows, and begged the trees to grow their branches into the little round room and the birds to come and live in it. And soon you could hardly see the ivory walls for green boughs and sweet-smelling flowers and luscious fruit; and the little birds came inside and built their nests there, and sang joyously together every morning and evening, and laid their eggs and fed their babies and taught them how to fly; and bees and moths and butterflies flitted in and out.

And now the Princess was so happy in her little round room that she quite forgot Golden Land.

There was only one thing she did not like about the little room, and that was that spiders lived there.

"It would be the loveliest room in the world without the spiders, Nurse," she said. "Couldn't we ask them to go somewhere else to live?"

"No," the Fairy Nurse replied. "The little round room at the top of the tower is the proper place for spiders."

"What are they there for, Nurse?" the Princess asked.

"To teach you how to spin," replied the Fairy Nurse.

Then the Princess remembered that her golden hair would not grow again until she had learnt to spin. So she sat down on the stool before the spinning-wheel and watched the spiders at work.

Until now she had always thought the spiders ugly and their webs gloomy and grey. But as she watched them she saw how patient and skilful they were, and how exquisitely soft and fine and silken were the strong grey threads they spun, and how marvellously and delicately they wove them into daintily patterned webs. And she found she could not dislike them any longer.

And the more she admired what was beautiful in the spiders and forgot what was ugly, and the harder she tried to spin as well as they did, the better spinner did

11

she become and the more her spinning-wheel seemed to whirl round all by itself.

And her golden hair began to grow again, just as her Fairy Nurse had said it would.

All twelve windows in the little round room were always wide open, and her little friends the birds were continually flying in with something new for her to spin. They brought her bits of everything — feathers and fur and leaves and flowers and grass and straw, and twigs and seeds and gossamer and dandelion clocks and tufts of bog-cotton, and even drops of dew and sap and mouthfuls of sweet nectar from the blossoms. And the Princess brought it all to her spinning-wheel and set it whirling and drew out a long silk thread; and at first the silken thread was grey, like the threads spun by the spiders, but presently it turned to shining gold.

And the more the Princess's spinning-wheel turned everything to gold, the longer grew her golden hair.

Now far away at the edge of the Great Forest there was a mill, and the miller had a son. The Miller's Son was very big and strong and sturdy; and the miller used to scold him because he did not use his strength working in the mill, but preferred to lie in the sun and watch the mill-stream flowing and gather the healing herbs which grew along its banks.

"What is the mill-stone for," the miller used to ask him impatiently, "if not for grinding corn?"

"I don't know yet," the Miller's Son would answer. "But I'm sure it *is* for something else."

One day, while he was lying in the sun and watching the mill-stream flowing, he noticed growing on its bank a beautiful blue flower which he had never seen before. He leaned over and plucked it, and out of the stem ran a white juice, like milk, making his finger-tips tingle. He put them to his mouth and sucked them to stop them tingling, and tasted on them the bitter taste of the milk of the blue flower; and straightaway he became aware of voices in the branches high above him.

He looked up, wondering who could be there; but there was nobody there at all except three ravens.

"It is a pity," said the first raven, "that the Miller's Son wastes his strength here when he could be using it to win the Princess in the Ivory Tower."

"His strength would not be enough to win her," said the second raven, "unless he had wisdom and kindness as well."

"He would need something else," said the third raven, "besides strength and wisdom and kindness. He would need the mill-stone which is the Ring of Destiny."

As soon as the Miller's Son heard the ravens mention the Princess in the Ivory Tower, there was nothing in all the world he wanted so much as to go at once and seek her. He rose from the grass and went to the whirling mill-stone, and he put his strong arms around it and heaved; and it came away, heavy though it was, and it went on whirling, and growing smaller as it whirled, till it was just a narrow stone ring. Then he slipped it on his little finger, and it ceased whirling.

"*Now* I know what the mill-stone is really for," said the Miller's Son. "Thank you, kind ravens!"

The three ravens were surprised and pleased when they saw the Miller's Son pick up the mill-stone and when he spoke to them in their own language.

"You are the first Miller's Son we have met who was wise," the first raven said, "and the first who knew our language."

"You must have tasted the Milk of the Golden Age which is stored in the stem of the Blue Flower," said the second raven.

And the third raven said:

"We would like to come with you."

"Come with pleasure," said the Miller's Son.

So they showed him which path of the many paths through the Great Forest he must follow, and the Miller's Son and the three ravens set out together to find the ivory tower.

They had not gone far when the Miller's Son heard a voice coming from a thicket, calling out for help. He turned aside from the path and went toward it; and there he found a leopard struggling in a trap.

"Lie still," said the Miller's Son, "and I will help you."

He opened the teeth of the trap and lifted the leopard free, and then he bathed the leopard's wounded leg at a little stream which ran by. And the leopard licked his hand in gratitude, and said:

"You are the first Miller's Son I have met who was kind, and the first who knew my language. You must have tasted the Milk of the Golden Age which is stored in the stem of the Blue Flower. I would like to come with you."

"Come with pleasure," said the Miller's Son.

So the Miller's Son and the leopard and the three ravens went on through the Great Forest together. They had not gone far when the Miller's Son heard a tremendous crash among the trees, and then a moaning voice calling out for help. He turned aside from the path and went toward it; and there he found a stag with his antlers pinned down by the branches of a fallen tree which had crashed across his path.

"Lie still," said the Miller's Son, "and I will help you."

Then the Miller's Son put forth all his strength, and heaved at the tree until it slowly lifted. And the stag rose from the ground with his antlers unharmed, and rubbed his head against the Miller's Son in gratitude, and said:

"You are the first Miller's Son I have met who was strong, and the first who knew my language. You must have tasted the Milk of the Golden Age which is stored in the stem of the Blue Flower. I would like to come with you."

"Come with pleasure," said the Miller's Son.

So the Miller's Son and the stag and the leopard and the three ravens went on through the Great Forest together. And at last they came to a clearing; and in the clearing was a tall tower of ivory.

The leopard and the stag and the three ravens stayed at the edge of the clearing; and the Miller's Son, with his heart beating very loudly, went to the tower of ivory and knocked upon the door.

Nobody came, so he knocked again. Still nobody came, so he knocked a third time. And he never saw the door open, but quite suddenly open it was, and there stood the Fairy Nurse, waiting.

"I am the Miller's Son," said the Miller's Son, "and I have come to win the Princess."

Now the Fairy Nurse was glad to see the Miller's Son, because she thought that it was quite time that somebody won the Princess. But she knew that before the Miller's Son could marry the Princess, he had to prove that he was the right kind of Miller's Son.

So she said to him:

"He who would marry the Princess must go through fire to win her."

"I am ready to do that," said the Miller's Son.

"Go back now to your companions," said the Fairy Nurse. "And tomorrow you can try."

So the Miller's Son went back to his companions and spent the night with them on the edge of the clearing. And when he woke next morning, there was a ring of fire burning between himself and the ivory tower.

He walked all round the ring of fire, but nowhere could he find any way of getting through. Then at last, the leopard said:

"Keep close behind me, and I will make a way through."

Then the leopard filled his mighty lungs with air, and went on filling them and filling them until it seemed there could not be any more air left in the world. Then he lowered his head, and thrust himself through the fire with a tremendous roaring; and the rush of his breath blew the fire to left and right, so that for an instant there was a lane between the flames. And along this lane the Miller's Son and the stag and the three ravens passed in safety.

The leopard's beautiful coat was scorched in many places; but the Miller's Son took from his breast the healing herbs which he had gathered as he lay in the sun by the mill-stream, and he laid them on the leopard's burns, and straight away the leopard was healed.

Then, with his heart beating very loudly, the Miller's Son went to the tower of ivory, and knocked upon the door.

Nobody came, so he knocked again. Still nobody came, so he knocked a third time. And he never saw the door open, but quite suddenly open it was, and there stood the Fairy Nurse, waiting.

"I am the Miller's Son," said the Miller's Son, "and I have gone through fire to win the Princess."

"You have done well," said the Fairy Nurse. "But he who would marry the Princess must also go through earth to win her."

"I am ready to do that," said the Miller's Son.

"Go back now to your companions," said the Fairy Nurse. "And tomorrow you can try."

So the Miller's Son went back to his companions, and spent the night with them half-way across the clearing. And when he woke next morning, there was a thick tangle of briars between himself and the ivory tower.

He walked all round the tangle of briars, but nowhere could he find any way of getting through. Then at last the three ravens said:

"Keep close behind us, and we will make a way through."

Then the three ravens flew right into the tangle of briars, and they tore off the thorns with their beaks and their claws, and they beat down the stems with their wings, until they had made a way along which the Miller's Son and the stag and the leopard passed in safety.

The ravens had lost their sleek and glossy plumage and were torn and bleeding all over; but the Miller's Son took from his breast the healing herbs which he had gathered as he lay in the sun by the mill-stream, and he laid them on the ravens' wounds, and straight away the ravens were healed.

Then, with his heart beating very loudly, the Miller's Son went to the tower of ivory, and knocked upon the door.

Nobody came, so he knocked again. Still nobody came, so he knocked a third time. And he never saw the door open, but quite suddenly open it was, and there stood the Fairy Nurse, waiting.

"I am the Miller's Son," said the Miller's Son, "and I have gone through both fire and earth to win the Princess."

"You have done well," said the Fairy Nurse. "But he who would marry the Princess must also go through water to win her."

"I am ready to do that," said the Miller's Son.

"Go back now to your companions," said the Fairy Nurse. "And tomorrow you can try."

So the Miller's Son went back to his companions, and spent the night with them. And when he woke next morning, there was a wide river flowing between himself and the ivory tower.

He went all along its bank, but nowhere could he find any way of getting over. Then at last the stag said:

"Lie in the water with your arm about my neck, and I will take you over."

So the Miller's Son lay in the water with his arm round the stag's neck, and the stag began to swim across the river. The water grew deeper and deeper, and the current grew stronger and stronger, and the stag sank lower and lower beneath the ripples until only his antlers were showing. But at last he brought the Miller's Son in safety to the other side. Then he went back to help the leopard; and the three ravens perched on his antlers and rode across the river with him.

When they were all safely over, the stag was spent and weary; but the Miller's Son took from his breast the healing herbs which he had gathered as he lay in the sun by the mill-stream, and he laid them on the stag's mouth and on his nostrils, and straight away the stag was healed.

Then, with his heart beating very loudly, the Miller's Son went to the tower of ivory, and knocked upon the door.

Nobody came, so he knocked again. Still nobody came, so he knocked a third time. And he never saw the door open, but quite suddenly open it was, and there stood the Fairy Nurse, waiting.

"I am the Miller's Son," said the Miller's Son, "and I have gone through fire and earth and water to win the Princess."

"You have done well," said the Fairy Nurse. "Go back now to your companions, and tomorrow you shall enter the ivory tower."

So the Miller's Son went back to his companions, and he and the stag and the leopard lay down to sleep. But the ravens were restless and wide awake. And the first raven said:

"It is strange that the Miller's Son did not also have to go through air to win the Princess."

And the second raven said:

"Perhaps the Fairy Nurse has still more tests in store for him."

And the third raven said:

"Let us stay awake tonight, and see what we can discover."

When the Miller's Son woke next morning, the three ravens came to him.

The first raven said:

"The Princess sits alone in a little round room at the top of the tower, and she spins everything in the whole world into gold. The Fairy Nurse will try to lead you the wrong way, but remember that you must go up and up the winding staircase if you would find the Princess."

Then the second raven said:

"But be careful, Miller's Son, when you come into the presence of the Princess. For she is so gloriously beautiful, and her golden hair is so dazzling, and the heaps of spun gold around her are so blinding, that she will take your breath away. And if you hold your breath only for as long as twelve heart-beats, forgetting to slip at once the Ring of Destiny on to her finger, she will be lost to you for ever."

And the third raven said:

"The Princess is so beautiful that even though we have warned you, it is still possible that you may forget. If you do, we ravens will peck your brow with our beaks, and the leopard must scratch you fiercely with his claws, and the stag must drive you forward with his antlers, to try to waken you out of your breathless trance."

The Miller's Son thanked the three ravens; then with his heart beating louder than ever, he went to the ivory tower. And this time the door stood open.

The Fairy Nurse was waiting for the Miller's Son, and she asked him to follow her. But she began to lead him the wrong way, toward a winding staircase which went down and down.

So the Miller's Son said firmly:

"*That* is not the right way to the Princess."

Then the Fairy Nurse asked:

"Which *is* the right way to the Princess, Miller's Son?"

And the Miller's Son replied:

"The winding staircase which goes up and up."

"Then where *is* the Princess, Miller's Son?" asked the Fairy Nurse.

And the Miller's Son said:

"She is spinning in the little round room at the top of the tower."

The Fairy Nurse smiled at him, because now he had proved quite clearly that he was the right kind of Miller's Son. And she led him the right way, up and up the winding staircase which led to the little round room. And the leopard and the stag and the three ravens followed very close behind him.

When the Fairy Nurse opened the door of the little round room, and the beauty of the Princess and the brightness of her golden hair and of the heaps of spun gold round her burst upon him, the Miller's Son was so dazzled and entranced that it took his breath away. He could do nothing but stand and stare at her, and he utterly forgot about the Ring of Destiny.

Then the three ravens rose on their dusky wings and pecked sharply at his brow; and the leopard scratched his breast fiercely with his claws; and the stag drove him forward with his powerful antlers. And just in time, just before the twelfth heart-beat, the Miller's Son began to breathe again, and woke up out of his trance, and remembered the raven's warning, and slipped the Ring of Destiny off his own finger and on to the finger of the Princess.

So the Princess and the Miller's Son were married, and lived together in great happiness in the ivory tower, with the Fairy Nurse to take care of them.

Every day the Princess spun more gold, and every morning the Miller's Son woke to find a golden coin under his pillow. And the stag and the leopard and the three ravens went out every day into the Great Forest to discover where there were poor wood-cutters and charcoal-burners in need of help. Then the Princess and the Miller's Son would take their gold to them, so that soon everywhere throughout the Great Forest all poor people blessed their names.

And a beautiful rose-coloured light began to shine round the ivory tower, glowing like a comforting beacon when wayfarers were astray in the dark.

So the Princess and the Miller's Son lived happily together year after year. And all the time the Princess's golden hair was growing longer, until one day she said:

"Look, Nurse! Look, dear Miller's Son!"

And when the Fairy Nurse and the Miller's Son looked, they saw that the Princess had let down her hair. It fell round her like a cloak made out of sunlight. And it had grown so long that it quite touched the ground.

Then the Fairy Nurse said: "When the Princess's hair touches the ground, then it is time to leave the ivory tower and go back to Golden Land."

So the Fairy Nurse wove together the rays of the rose-coloured light which shone about the tower, so that they were wrapped like a fairy web about the Princess and the Miller's Son and herself and the stag and the leopard and the three ravens and the little birds who had helped the Princess with her spinning.

And on the fairy web of rose-coloured light they all rose high above the ivory tower; and as they looked down at it they saw it begin to shrink and fall and crumble, till at last it was just a heap of white dust in the clearing in the forest.

They watched while the wind softly carried the white dust among the trees, where the moss and the grasses opened happy green arms to receive it. Then the fairy web of rose-coloured light began to float gently away over the tree-tops, bearing them away from the Great Forest toward Golden Land, where the King and Queen lovingly awaited their homecoming.

# The Fox who went to Heaven

Raginohart the Fox was the cleverest animal in the Forest; indeed, that was why he was called Raginohart, which means "strong through cunning."

He was the sprucest and best groomed of the animals, too, with his long, neat muzzle, his bright, quick eyes, his gleaming red-brown coat, and his magnificent bushy brush. He was very light and sure on his feet, and very brisk and swift in his movements.

In fact, he was full of Forest virtues.

But he was also conceited, and looked down on less gifted animals. And his glossy coat covered a heart of stone.

One evening, toward supper-time, Raginohart strolled out to visit a farm-yard on the edge of the Forest, where there lived a fine, plump young hen about whom Raginohart had for some weeks been thinking lovingly at this hour of the day.

Just as he had expected, there was the fine, plump young hen roosting in a tree, her eyes already drowsily half-closed.

"Good evening! Good evening!" said Raginohart heartily, bowing in a very polished fashion. "What a beautiful picture you make up there, dear Hen! And what an excellent climber you must be to climb such a difficult tree! I doubt if *I* could climb it!"

"Oh, I did not climb it sir — I flew," said the innocent young hen, bobbing Raginohart a curtsey, and thinking that there was not one animal in the farm-yard who had such exquisite manners.

"You flew?" repeated Raginohart, apparently in surprise. "How is it then that I have never seen you flying in the Forest?"

"Oh, sir," the little hen explained, "my wings are not really flying wings. They will carry me just up here to roost; but they would never carry me through the Forest."

"What a pity," said Raginohart, shaking his head sadly, "when there are all manner of marvels to be seen there! You would like to see them, wouldn't you?"

"Indeed, indeed I would, sir," said the little hen longingly.

"Then you shall come for a ride through the Forest on my brush," said Raginohart, brightening. "I run like the wind; so you will know what it feels like to be really flying, *and* you will see all the marvels of the Forest, too."

So the cunning Raginohart stretched out his fine, bushy brush; and the innocent little hen, flattered to be noticed by such an elegant and courtly animal, fluttered down from the tree and perched on it. And off Raginohart went through the Forest, running like the wind.

"Are you enjoying it?" he called back to the little hen.

"Oh, sir, it is *wonderful!*" she replied, her little round eyes shining with excitement. "I never knew there were so many marvels in the Forest! And you go so swiftly that it is just as if I were flying for the first time in my life!"

"Spread out your wings," said Raginohart kindly, "and then it will be as if you were *really* flying."

So the innocent little hen spread out her wings, and in doing so she lost her balance and fell off Raginohart's brush. And *hey presto!* in a twinkle Raginohart had pounced on her and killed her.

Now it was one of the customs of the Forest for all the animals to forgather at the Sibyl's Bower when the sun went down, and to eat their evening meal together. And as Raginohart, carrying the plump little hen, made his way through the Forest toward the Sibyl's Bower, he fell in with Bruno the Bear.

Bruno was a great, shaggy, shabby, shuffling, shambling, untidy, clumsy creature; and the clever and elegant and nimble Raginohart loved to poke fun at his slow wits and moth-eaten coat and dreamy ways. But whereas Raginohart had a heart of stone under his glossy coat, Bruno under his moth-eaten one had a heart of gold. But Raginohart did not know what either heart was made of, for his eyes were so bright and sharp that they could see only the outside of things and not what was inside them.

"Good evening, Bruno mine," said Raginohart gaily. And because he was very pleased with his own wiliness, he told the bear the story of how he had snared the innocent little hen for his supper.

"Now, wasn't that very clever?" he asked when he had finished.

Beside him Bruno stumbled along on his short hind legs as if he were not quite happy.

"Yes, it was very *clever*, Raginohart," he agreed slowly. "Only — it wasn't quite *kind*, was it, to the little hen?"

Raginohart threw back his sleek, well-groomed head and laughed and laughed.

"Kind to the little hen?" he repeated. "A fox must eat!"

27

He looked up at Bruno, and saw that he was supper-less, so he went on teasingly:

"A bear must eat, too. How are you going to get *your* supper, Bruno, since you scorn to get it by cleverness, as I got mine?"

And Bruno answered very simply:

"I shall sing for it."

Again Raginohart threw back his head and laughed and laughed.

"*You* sing, you great gruff growler?" he mocked. "Who on earth is going to reward such singing as yours with a supper"

"Here we are, so you will see," replied Bruno, still in perfect good humour.

They had reached a hollow tree, from which came a sound like long, deep organ notes, which Raginohart recognized as the humming of a busy colony of bees. Bruno stood upright, facing the hole in the tree-trunk, and began to sing, hoarsely and gruffly and growlingly, just as Raginohart had said he would.

He made up the words as he went along; and this is what he sang:

> "Bees, dear bees of Paradise!
> Can you of your star-food spare
> For your friend, the big brown bear?
> Sweet gold for my evening fare,
> Bees, dear bees of Paradise?"

The bees did not seem to mind the gruffness of Bruno's singing, for the long, deep organ notes inside the hollow tree swelled louder and turned into words. And the words were these:

"Take, dear bear, your heavenly food,
But do not harm our sleeping brood.
Take the fruit of sun and star,
But come not where our nurselings are.
Of their waxen cribs take care;
But take your honey, dear brown bear!"

Then Bruno gently put his big, clumsy paw inside the hollow tree, and felt about very delicately. And when he carefully drew it out again, in it was a huge chunk of shining white honey-comb, with clear, thick, golden honey oozing slowly from the broken cells along the edge of it. Bruno stood quite still and sang again:

"Bees, dear bees of Paradise!
Thank you for my supper sweet.
God send you as good to eat,
Bees, dear bees of Paradise!"

Then, happily licking the falling drops of honey from the edges of the honey-comb, he shambled on his way beside the prancing Raginohart.

"I can't think how you can eat such stuff!" exclaimed Raginohart, wrinkling his long muzzle in distaste. "Give *me* good, strong flesh to eat! It tastes of earth. But what can your honey taste of?"

"It tastes of heaven," said Bruno very simply.

Raginohart sniffed his contempt, and went on finding fault with good-natured Bruno:

"You find your supper in hollow trees, and you make your bed in hollow trees. Why on earth you choose a hollow tree to live in I simply can't imagine. Why don't you live in a good rock cave, as I do? It does me good to sleep inside the cold, hard earth!"

"It does *me* good to sleep inside a tree that is warm and living," replied Bruno. "I should feel dead and buried if I slept in a cave as you do."

"And another thing," Raginohart went on, for it made him feel superior to find fault. "Why must you always be trying to walk on two legs, as that slow creature, Man, does? You would be much swifter and surer if you went on four legs, as I do, and all proper-thinking animals."

"The snake in my backbone likes to be lifted up," answered Bruno dreamily. "And that seems to matter more than being swift or sure."

There were plenty of other faults that Raginohart could have found with Bruno. He would have liked to tell him that his hair wanted combing and that his nails wanted cutting and that his coat wanted brushing and that his whole appearance was an absolute disgrace. But he could not because by now they had reached the Sibyl's Bower, and in the Sibyl's Bower the animals could say only kind things to one another.

The Sibyl's Bower was the most beautiful spot in all the Forest. The Sibyl had made the Bower herself by twining together the branches of living plants, so that the ceiling was made of leaves, which flooded the Bower beneath them with a soft green light during the day. And in spring sweet-scented flowers looked down from the ceiling of leaves, and in autumn ripe fruit hung thick from it.

The Sibyl was very wise. She listened to the wind in the trees, and to the stream which flowed through her Bower. And there was no secret that she did not know, for she possessed the Crystal of Truth.

At night, when the soft green light from the ceiling of leaves was dimmed, the Sibyl's Bower seemed filled with white daylight; this was the light of the Crystal of

Truth. And if you held the Crystal of Truth in your hands, you did not see things in their outward seeming, but you saw them as they really were inside their enchanted forms.

Each evening, as the animals of the Forest ate together in the Sibyl's Bower, and gathered on the hearth before her fire, and talked and played and told each other stories, the Sibyl sat apart at her loom, weaving a magic tapestry. She would look up now and again to speak a wise word or to tell a story herself, but she never stopped weaving. The magic tapestry went on growing day after day; but the Sibyl never seemed to come to the end of it.

Raginohart was a very inquisitive fox, and he often rose from his place before the fire and came across the Sibyl's Bower to look at the magic tapestry; but the pictures which the Sibyl was weaving did not much appeal to him. They seemed always to be pictures of men and women and angels in a strange land, a land he did not like because it seemed unearthly and he liked things to belong to the earth which he saw and smelt and felt and tasted every day.

Sometimes the Sibyl wove pictures in which these people were sitting at a banquet, dressed in golden robes, with jewelled girdles round their waists, and golden crowns on their heads, and on their breasts golden hearts which pulsed and shone. Bruno loved these scenes, but Raginohart thought the banquets very poor ones, for all the feast upon the table was only bread and wine and fish and honey.

But tonight, when Raginohart came across the Sibyl's Bower to look at the growing magic tapestry, his ears stood up with surprise and interest. For the Sibyl had woven a fox playing a lute. And yes, the longer

Raginohart looked at it, the more certain he was that it was a portrait of himself.

"Is that a picture of me, Sibyl?" he asked.

"It could be, Couldn't it?" said the Sibyl, looking up and smiling.

"No, it Couldn't, really," said Raginohart. "Not with that lute. You know I don't like music."

"But wouldn't it be lovely if you did!" the Sibyl murmured, sending her brightly coloured shuttle through the web. "Then you could play to us every evening. And how we should all love it!"

Raginohart liked the thought of being the centre of attraction, but he reminded her:

"But I don't know *how* to play!"

"But you are so clever, you would soon learn," said the Sibyl. "And you have such nimble paws, dear Fox — they are just made for playing a lute. Bruno, reach my lute down from that high branch, and let Raginohart try."

Now Raginohart felt very flattered when the Sibyl spoke of his cleverness. He was the only animal in the Forest who was clever enough to realize how clever the Sibyl herself was, though with quite a different cleverness from his own; but he had always had a rather aggrieved feeling that she did not value *his* cleverness enough.

So when Bruno staggered to the corner of the Sibyl's Bower, and reached up his clumsy paws, and took down the lute from the high branch from which it hung by its embroidered ribbon, Raginohart took it and slipped the ribbon around his neck and held it against his breast and began to pluck the strings.

And immediately he felt something strange happening in his breast, where the lute was pressing against it, as though a hard lump there were turning into something between light and water. It was really that the music of the lute was already beginning to melt his heart of stone.

The tunes which his nimble paws called forth from the lute were snippy, snappy little tunes, all points and angles and sharp corners, no smoothly flowing melodies.

Bruno, who was listening with his head dropped forward on his shaggy breast, opened his little eyes and blinked and groaned.

"Oh, Raginohart!" he growled dreamily. "You are playing knives and scissors and pins and pine-needles! They keep pricking and cutting me!"

"What *shall* I play, then?" asked Raginohart, a little huffily.

"Play something like this," said Bruno.

And in his funny, gruff singing voice he began to hum a strange, unearthly, haunting melody, which gave Raginohart the oddest sensation of growing bigger and bigger, right out of his skin, until he filled the Forest and reached right up to the stars.

"Stop, stop!" he cried angrily, for he did not like to feel outside himself like this. It made him feel unsure of himself, and feeling sure of himself was the feeling which of all feelings he liked best. "Stop, stop! Bruno, where on earth did you learn such a tune?"

"Nowhere on earth. In heaven," murmured Bruno drowsily, and fell fast asleep.

Raginohart sniffed, to show Bruno that he thought that an absurd remark for him to make, and glanced at the Sibyl, to see what *she* thought of it. But the Sibyl was working steadily at her weaving, sending her brightly coloured shuttle through the web, and did not seem to think Bruno had said anything odd at all.

Now one of Raginohart's many good points was that if he did a thing at all, he was willing to take a lot of trouble in order to do it well. So he took the lute back to his cave in order to learn to play it better, and he used often to play it when he was alone.

Sometimes he made up tunes to lure plump little hens from their roosts; but when he played these with great pride in the Sibyl's Bower at sunset, the smaller animals of the Forest did not like them. Now and again he would try to recapture that strange unearthly, haunting melody of Bruno's; but it always gave him that same feeling of growing out of his sleek, well-groomed pelt. So he always very quickly gave it up.

But even when he played only the snippy, snappy little tunes which came most easily to him, the tunes full of knives and scissors and pins and pine-needles, he felt again that new melting sensation in his breast.

So the year wore away, and the weather grew cold and the trees grew bare. And now there began to be gaps in the circle of animals round the fire in the Sibyl's Bower; for the hibernating ones, like the snakes and the dormice and the squirrels, had curled themselves up in their winter quarters and gone to sleep till spring.

To his surprise, Raginohart found that for the first time in his life he missed them. But the one he missed most was Bruno the Bear; for although he scoffed at him so much and had so many faults to find with him, yet he had a corner for him in his melting heart of stone.

Raginohart himself did not feel sleepy in winter. On the contrary, winter made him feel more awake than ever. So he still went to and fro about the Forest; and whenever his way led him near Bruno's hollow tree, he always stopped and looked in to see if Bruno showed any signs of waking. And always there was the big brown bear sleeping away so heavily that neither thunder nor storm nor even Raginohart's pinching and poking ever disturbed him.

One day at sunset toward the end of winter, Raginohart was approaching Bruno's hollow tree when he saw something so amazing that he could hardly believe his own sharp and clever eyes. For just leaving the hollow tree was the most magnificent fairy prince, dressed in golden robes, with a jewelled girdle round his waist and a golden sword hanging from it, with a golden crown on his head, and on his breast a golden heart pulsing and glowing so radiantly that it made a golden mist all about him.

Raginohart could not imagine why such a wonderful and exalted person should visit the shabby brown bear, and he was filled with the greatest surprise and curiosity. So he ran and looked into the hollow tree, meaning to ask Bruno all about it.

But, stranger than ever, there was Bruno, still fast asleep as he had been all winter. Raginohart shouted at him and tickled him and poked him and pinched him and pulled his ears and tried to lift his eyelids; but Bruno still slept on. He was so thoroughly sound asleep that Raginohart knew he could not possibly have wakened to receive the prince.

If once Raginohart scented any mystery, he could never rest until he had unravelled it. So next day, while the sun was still high in the sky, he went and lay in the bushes near Bruno's hollow tree, so that he might see the fairy prince arrive if he came again. Then, while the prince was inside the tree with Bruno, Raginohart meant to call upon his friend.

He peeped into the tree before he lay in the bushes, and there was Bruno, still fast asleep. All afternoon he watched and waited, but he saw no fairy prince arrive. And then, just as the sun was setting, he saw the fairy prince *come out* of the hollow tree and walk away through the Forest.

"How extraordinary!" thought Raginohart, really puzzled. "How on earth did he get in without my seeing him? And why on earth does he visit Bruno, when Bruno never wakes?"

Again he peeped inside the tree, and there was Bruno sleeping, just as he had seen him when he arrived to watch for the prince. Again he tried to waken him, and again Bruno just slept on.

And suddenly Raginohart realized something which made everything seem stranger than ever. He realized that Bruno was so big that he entirely filled the hollow trunk.

"There Isn't room *anywhere* in Bruno's tree for the prince," he thought. "And yet, with my own two sharp, clever eyes, I saw the prince come out of it!"

And then he thought:

"I wonder where the prince comes from? I wonder where he goes to?"

So next day he came and waited and watched again. Again he never saw the fairy prince enter the tree; but again, just as the sun was setting, he saw the prince come out of the tree and walk away through the Forest.

And this time Raginohart followed him.

The prince went on through the Forest to a part to which Raginohart had never been before. Here, where the trees stopped, there rose a high mountain.

The prince climbed the mountain, with Raginohart following him; and when he reached the summit, he stepped off on to steps of cloud.

The prince climbed the steps of cloud, up and up and

up, until at last he came to the golden gates of Heaven. They opened as the prince approached, and he went through them; then they closed fast behind, leaving Raginohart behind.

Raginohart peered through the bars, and saw a most strange and unearthly land, a land of delicate floating colours, as if rainbows had broken loose and were drifting everywhere. Everywhere was quite silent; and everywhere was bathed in a soft and tender golden haze.

Raginohart did not like it very much, for it was so unlike earth. But he was so very inquisitive that he thought he would like to go in, just to see what he could find out about Bruno's mysterious visitor.

So he knocked at the golden gates very loudly. And St Peter got up from his golden rock and came toward the gates.

"I want to come in," said Raginohart, haughtily.

"I'm sorry, but at present you can't," said St Peter very kindly. "It's awfully hard, at any time, for little tailors to get into Heaven."

Raginohart wondered why St Peter should mistake a fox for a little tailor. At any other time he would at once have asked him why, but now he was too deeply offended to ask any questions. Without another word he lifted his muzzle high in the air, and turned and stalked away in dignified silence.

As he came down the steps of cloud and down the mountain, it seemed to him that he must have been away a very long time, for warm breezes met him, and the trees were putting forth leaf-buds, and bulbs were putting forth flower-buds, and everywhere there were signs that the spring had arrived.

"Bruno will soon be awake again," thought

Raginohart. "Perhaps he will come to the Sibyl's Bower tonight!"

And at the pleasure he felt at the prospect of talking with Bruno again, the stone which was his heart melted a little more.

When Raginohart came that evening to the Sibyl's Bower, the Sibyl was working at her magic tapestry, and he went to look at it. And again his ears stood up in surprise and interest; for now he recognized the strange, unearthly land in her pictures. It was the very land he had seen last night through the golden gates of Heaven.

Then he looked again, and again his ears were pricked with even greater surprise and interest. For the prince she had just finished weaving, the prince sitting at a banquet of bread and wine and fish and honey, was no other than Bruno's prince himself!

"Is that a picture of Bruno's prince, Sibyl?" he asked.

"It could be, Couldn't it?" she said, looking up and smiling.

"There's a mystery about that prince," said Raginohart.

"There are many mysteries about every prince," the Sibyl murmured, sending her brightly coloured shuttle through the web.

"But the biggest mystery of all," went on Raginohart, "is how he gets inside the tree when Bruno's there. There simply Isn't room for two."

"There wouldn't need to be, would there," smiled the Sibyl, "if the two were really one?"

"The two really one?" echoed Raginohart, mystified. Then he saw what the Sibyl meant; for he really was a clever fox, with thoughts as swift and nimble as his feet. "You mean — Bruno *is* the fairy prince?"

And just then Bruno came in, still drowsy from his long winter sleep.

Raginohart watched him shuffling along, shabby, clumsy, stumbling, his pelt all tattered and torn. And he marvelled how anyone as wise as the Sibyl was could possibly suggest that such a rag-tag-and-bobtail tatterdemalion could be the handsome, graceful, gold-clad fairy prince.

Raginohart sniffed a gigantic sniff, to show how absurd he found the suggestion; but when he turned back to the Sibyl, she was regarding him with her wise and quiet smile.

"Take the Crystal of Truth in your paw," the Sibyl whispered. "And then look at Bruno again."

Raginohart felt that if he did not unravel this mystery he would die of curiosity. So he went across the Sibyl's Bower to the great stone on which the Crystal of Truth was kept; and he took the Crystal of Truth in his paw, and fixed his sharp, bright eyes on Bruno.

For a moment Raginohart was blinded by the crystal's clear, white light, brighter than any daylight. Then the shabby, clumsy bear was there no longer; but in his place stood the fairy prince, dressed in golden robes, with the jewelled girdle around his waist and the golden sword at his side, a golden crown upon his head, and upon his breast a heart of glowing, pulsing gold.

And while Raginohart stood gazing and gasping, hardly able to believe his own sharp, bright eyes, the Sibyl whispered again:

"And now look at yourself *in* the Crystal of Truth."

Raginohart looked at himself in the Crystal of Truth, and he felt very proud of the elegant and gentlemanly fox he saw there. Then again he was blinded for a moment by the crystal's clear, white light, brighter than any daylight. And then the sleek pelt and the long muzzle and the big, bushy brush disappeared, and there stood a little tailor in a grey jerkin, with shrewd, bright eyes and a long, inquisitive nose and nimble fingers and a great pair of scissors stuck into his belt.

Bruno a fairy prince and himself a little tailor? Raginohart's pride would not allow him to believe it. But as he gazed, spellbound, at the long-nosed, bright-eyed little tailor, he began to see that he was a tremendously clever fellow. Yes, in *that* way the little tailor *was* like the wonderful Raginohart, after all!

And then Raginohart thought of a clever way of finding out if the Crystal of Truth was really telling the truth.

While Raginohart had been gazing at the little tailor in the crystal, the fairy prince had become a bear again. So now Raginohart, still looking into the crystal, snatched the big scissors from his belt, and dashed across the Sibyl's Bower, and slashed open the front of Bruno's tattered pelt.

And there, through the gaping bear-skin, he caught a glimpse of a golden robe, and a jewelled girdle, and a heart of glowing, pulsing gold.

"Oh dear, what a bundle of rags I am," said Bruno mildly, blinking down at himself. "I *do* need a needle and thread!"

"Dear Fox," said the Sibyl quietly, "you must sew the bear-skin together again."

So the little tailor took a needle and thread from the front of his jerkin and sewed the rent together. And he did it so skilfully that you could not tell the bear-skin had been cut at all.

"That is quite perfect, Raginohart," the Sibyl praised him. "You certainly *are* a clever little tailor!"

And the way in which she said it, and Bruno's pleasure in the beautiful mending of his pelt, and his own joy in doing the mending beautifully melted the stone in Raginohart's breast a little more yet.

"So St Peter was right, after all, when he called me a little tailor," said Raginohart. "But I wonder why he wouldn't let me enter Heaven?"

"Why did you want to enter Heaven?" the Sibyl asked him.

"Out of curiosity," replied Raginohart.

"That's why you Couldn't," said the Sibyl. "That's why St Peter said you Couldn't *at present*."

"But I'd like to enter for another reason now," went on Raginohart.

"And what is that?" asked the Sibyl.

"To be there with Bruno," said Raginohart.

"Then try again," smiled the Sibyl.

So the next evening, when at sunset Bruno turned into the fairy prince, Raginohart turned into a little tailor, and together they went to the edge of the Forest, and climbed the high mountain and the steps of cloud to the golden gates of Heaven. And the golden gates flew open to let the prince come in; but they clashed together again in the face of the little tailor.

"Please may I come in?" asked the little tailor humbly. He did not say "I want to," haughtily, as he did the first time.

St Peter was sitting on his golden rock, and St John was standing beside him, talking, with a pen made out of an angel's feather in his hand and his eagle on his shoulder.

"I'm afraid that first you must show us what you can do," St John said very kindly. The little tailor looked about for something that would help him to show how

42

clever he was. First he saw a little naked child standing close to him and gazing wistfully up into his face. But he did not see how she could help him to show how clever he was, so he looked away.

Then he saw the Cloths of Twilight hanging, the most beautiful cloths in the whole world, cloths of gauze and silk and velvet, blue and purple and dove-grey.

And as soon as he saw the Cloths of Twilight, Raginohart knew what he could do to show how clever he was.

Out came his great scissors from his belt, and snip, snip, snip, snip, *snip*, they went, this way and that, in a gay, mad, sparkling dance of cuts and slashes, till half of the Cloths of Twilight lay in shreds and snippets, all most elegantly shaped, all over the clouds in front of the golden gates.

"He certainly *is* a clever little tailor!" exclaimed St Peter enthusiastically. "The flash of those scissors was like sword-play! Don't you think that we might let him in?"

"Oh Peter, how you do love sword-play!" St John said, smiling. "Don't you see that the little tailor is so clever that he would wreck Heaven if we let him in? It will need a whole company of angels working night and day, as it is, to make the Cloths of Twilight whole again. And how many more would it not need to make *Heaven* whole again if those clever scissors began madly snipping at the sun and moon and stars?"

So Raginohart turned away from the golden gates again. But this time he went down the steps of cloud and the mountain not in offended pride but in sadness.

For Heaven no longer seemed to him a strange place which he did not like very much. He was beginning to be as homesick for Heaven as if Heaven were earth. And his homesickness for Heaven made the stone heart in his breast melt more and more.

Raginohart went to the Sibyl's Bower, and told the Sibyl all that had happened. She was silent till all was told; then she asked:

"What good were the Cloths of Twilight when you had cut them into snippets?"

"No good at all," said Raginohart.

Then the Sibyl asked another question:

"What did you do when you had cut Bruno's bear-skin?"

"Sewed it up again," said Raginohart.

Then the Sibyl said no more, but went on with her magic tapestry, sending her brightly coloured shuttle through the web. And Raginohart looked at the picture she was weaving, and it was a picture of a little tailor and a naked child who was gazing wistfully up into his face. And suddenly his melting heart told him what to do next time.

And the next evening, when again he climbed the steps of cloud with Bruno, and again the golden gates opened for the prince but not for him, he looked about him and saw once more the little naked child gazing wistfully up into his face. And this time he smiled at her, and chose the most beautiful of all the Cloths of Twilight, the one of soft blue silk; and from it, with his clever scissors, he carefully cut out a little garment. And he sewed it together with most loving skill. And then he put it on the little naked child.

And the child smiled back at him, and put her hand in his, and led him to the golden gates. And the gates opened and let them both in. And St Peter and St John smiled in friendly fashion, and welcomed the little tailor into Heaven.

Then Raginohart stood amazed. For it had been quite, quite silent everywhere when he stood outside the golden gates. But as soon as he entered Heaven, it was just as if everything burst out singing.

The grass was singing and the corn was singing, the trees were singing and the flowers were singing and the fruits were singing, the air was singing, the sun was singing, the streams were singing, the very ground was singing. And everywhere there were angels with harps and shawms and dulcimers, playing to the singing.

And the melody was the one which Bruno had sung to him.

A long, long way off, Raginohart could see the fairy prince seated at a banquet. Nobody asked the little tailor to come to the table and eat. At one time Raginohart would have been offended, but now he did not mind. He felt very humble, and very happy, and very, very, grateful that he had been allowed to enter Heaven at all.

When he said this to the Sibyl on his return to the Forest, she smiled a most beautiful smile.

"Those who feast in Heaven are those who have helped to fashion Heaven," she said.

Then she was silent and went on working at her magic tapestry. And when Raginohart looked at the picture she was weaving, he saw it was a picture of a little tailor playing on a lute.

Then Raginohart went back to his cave, and he took down the Sibyl's lute from its rocky shelf, and he began to play the heavenly melody which Bruno had once sung to him.

And as he played it he began to grow and grow, till he left his fox-skin far away below him, and he found himself before the golden gates. And they opened to him. And he went in and sat down on the heavenly lawns near the angels who were playing their harps and shawms and dulcimers. And he began to play his lute with them.

And they all looked at him and smiled, and nodded a friendly greeting as if to an old comrade. And the stone in his breast melted quite away, and the place where it had been grew warm and glowing. And he felt as if he had all his life been wandering and had now at last come home.

And when he came back to the Forest and went to the Sibyl's Bower, the Sibyl held out both her hands to him in welcome and kissed him on the brow.

And when he looked at her magic tapestry, he saw a woven picture of a little tailor dressed as royally as any prince; and on his breast there glowed and pulsed a heart of gold. And he sat at the banquet beside the other prince, his friend. And they were both eating honey.

# The White Doe

There was once a Prince who lived very happily in his father's castle, spending his whole time hunting in the forest. The King and Queen thought that he was quite old enough to marry, and they wanted him to visit other Kings in other kingdoms and choose a princess for his bride. But the Prince was so content with his life in his father's kingdom that he could not bring himself to leave it.

One day he was out in the forest, hunting, with his huntsmen and attendants, when a noble white doe bounded across his path. The Prince turned aside to pursue her; and presently, ahead in a clearing, he saw her standing at bay, with the royal hounds encircling her. But the strange thing was that the hounds were not attacking her, but were standing back from her with great respect.

Even from a distance the Prince could see the flashing of something golden on her brow; and he urged his horse forward, and beat off the hounds, and bent down to look more closely. She lifted her head and looked at him imploringly; and he saw that she bore on her brow a picture of a Princess, framed in a heart-shaped frame of gold set with tiny perfect pearls.

And the Princess in the picture was so lovely that the Prince loved her there and then with his whole heart.

By now the Prince's attendants had galloped after him, and he looked round at them and asked:

"Is any story told of this White Doe?"

And the Chief Huntsman, who had grown old in the forest and knew its stories and was wise in all its ways, nodded and said:

"Your Royal Highness, the forest folk say that neither spear nor hound can wound her, and that it is her fate to dwell in the forest and be hunted until a Prince shall fall in love with the picture she bears on her brow."

The Prince thought to himself:

"That has already happened!"

But aloud he asked:

"Who is this Princess? And where lies her father's kingdom?"

And the Chief Huntsman answered:

"Your Royal Highness, that is a secret which is known to none of the forest folk. But it is said that when the Prince who is to be the Princess's true lover shall fall in love with the picture, then the White Doe herself will show him the way to the Princess."

Then the Prince dismounted straight away, and took his ring from his finger, and gave it to his attendants, and said to them:

"Take this ring to the King and Queen, my parents, and with it tidings to make glad their hearts; tidings that I have departed to do that which they have so long wished — to seek a bride."

His horse and his spear and his hunting-horn he bade them take back to his father's castle. And then he said farewell.

Clad just as he was, in his plain green hunting tabard, he laid his hand gently on the neck of the White Doe; and she lifted her head and chose a path toward the north; and side by side, and with no one else with them, they went together through the forest.

Presently they came forth from the forest into a valley strewn with rocks. It was a strange valley, where nothing green grew except prickly cactus-plants, and it was netted with narrow winding pathways. Here and there they saw enormous spiders scurrying over the boulders, and curious bull-like creatures feeding on the cactus-plants. But none harmed them.

For many days the Prince and the White Doe travelled together across this valley, till at last they came to a group of standing-stones, into which other stones had been built to form a house of rock. It had a cunningly-wrought door of maple-wood, and on the door was a knocker of brilliant black tin-stone, shaped like a figure four.

And the White Doe stopped before the door, and turned her head, and looked at the Prince imploringly.

So the Prince stepped up to the door, and lifted the knocker, and knocked three times. And the door opened, and there stood a little grey man with a pair of scissors of brilliant white metal in his hand. And the front of his grey tunic was full of needles, each threaded with a black thread.

The little grey man listened while the Prince told him his story, and did not say a word. Then the Prince said:

"It is in my mind that the White Doe led me to your house that you might show me the way to the Princess."

But the little grey man shook his head as he replied:

"No, I cannot show you the way to the Princess. Only the White Doe can do that. But look at the Princess's picture. Can you not see something amiss?"

The Prince looked at the picture, and he saw that it had been spotted by the rain and faded by the sun and scratched by the cactus-plants and grimed by the dust of the valley.

Then the little grey man said:

"The White Doe led you to my house because if the picture of the Princess is spoilt further she can no longer find the way to her."

Then the Prince asked the little grey man:

"What can I do to protect the picture?"

And the little grey man replied:

"You can sew a magic cover for it. Only the cover must be as clear and transparent as glass; because if you could no longer see the picture, then you would forget all about the Princess, and give up your search for her."

Then the Prince asked:

"What could such a magic cover be sewn with?"

And the little grey man replied:

"Only with white nettles."

Then the Prince asked eagerly:

"Where can I learn to make such a magic cover?"

And the little grey man replied:

"I am a tailor, and I know the secret. But it will take seven years to teach you."

Now the Prince thought such a secret was well worth seven years' study, so he stayed seven years with the Tailor, in the house of the standing-stones. And the White Doe stayed with him.

And he learned everything that the Tailor could teach him; and at last he was able to make a cover of white nettles which was as clear and transparent as glass for the picture of the Princess.

And the Prince was no older at the end of the seven years with the Tailor than he had been at the beginning.

Then he said farewell to the Tailor, and the Tailor gave him a walnut as wages for his seven years' work. And the Tailor said:

"Keep it carefully, and do not crack it until you find yourself in grievous need of a tailor's skill."

The Prince thanked the Tailor and put the walnut away in his pouch. Then he set out from the house of standing-stones with his hand resting gently on the neck of the White Doe. And protecting the picture of the Princess on her brow was the cover made of white nettles which was as clear and transparent as glass.

And the White Doe lifted her head and chose a path toward the east; and side by side, and with no one else with them, they followed it until they came forth out of the valley of rocks and saw before them a high mountain.

Together the Prince and the White Doe climbed the mountain. It was a strange mountain, with yawning abysses and fissures in the ground, from which issued mist and smoke and sometimes flame; and its peak was a volcano crater, bubbling and seething like a witch's cauldron. Among the streams of frozen lava on the mountain's side they saw snakes and scorpions. But none harmed them.

For many days the Prince and the White Doe travelled together over this mountain, till at last, on the further slope, they came to a cave. It had a mighty door of oak, and on the door was a heavy iron knocker, shaped like an arrow.

And the White Doe stopped before the door, and turned her head, and looked at the Prince imploringly.

So the Prince stepped up to the door, and lifted the knocker, and knocked three times. And the door opened, and there, in the glow of a great, roaring fire, stood a black giant in a huge apron of blood-red leather, an enormous iron hammer in his enormous hand.

The black giant listened while the Prince told him his story, and did not say a word. Then the Prince said:

"It is in my mind that the White Doe led me to your cave that you might show me the way to the Princess."

But the black giant shook his head as he replied:

"No, I cannot show you the way to the Princess. Only the White Doe can do that. But look at the White Doe's feet. Can you not see something amiss?"

The Prince gently lifted the White Doe's left forefoot and examined it. And he found that it was raw and tender and bleeding, and that the horn was worn away right to the flesh. And he looked at the other three feet; and they were all the same.

Then the black giant said:

"The White Doe led you to my cave because if her feet suffer further she will be lamed and can no longer show you the way to the Princess."

Then the Prince asked the black giant:

"What can I do to protect the White Doe's feet?"

And the black giant replied:

"You can forge magic shoes for them. Only the shoes must be as light as thistledown; because otherwise she could not lift such delicate feet at all, and so you would have to give up your search for the Princess."

Then the Prince asked:

"What could such magic shoes be made of?"

And the black giant replied:

"Only of quicksilver."

Then the Prince asked eagerly:

"Where can I learn to make such magic shoes?"

And the black giant replied:

"I am a smith, and I know the secret. But it will take seven years to teach you."

Now the Prince thought such a secret was well worth

seven years' study, so he stayed the seven years with the Smith, in the cave of the roaring fire. And the White Doe stayed with him.

And he learned everything that the Smith could teach him; and at last he was able to forge shoes of quicksilver which were as light as thistledown for the feet of the White Doe.

And the Prince was no older at the end of the seven years with the Smith than he had been at the beginning.

Then he said farewell to the Smith, and the Smith gave him a monkey-nut as wages for his seven years' work. And the Smith said:

"Keep it carefully, and do not crack it until you find yourself in grievous need of a smith's skill."

The Prince thanked the Smith, and put the monkey-nut away in his pouch with the Tailor's walnut. Then he set out from the cave of the roaring fire with his hand resting gently on the neck of the White Doe. And protecting the picture of the Princess on her brow was the cover made of white nettles which was as clear and transparent as glass; and protecting her feet were the shoes of quicksilver which were as light as thistledown.

And the White Doe lifted her head and chose a path toward the south; and side by side, and with no one else with them, they followed it until they came down to the foot of the mountain and saw before them a wide swamp.

Together the Prince and the White Doe crossed the swamp. It was a strange swamp, with livid pools, and patches of coarse purple grass, and leaning trees with twisted roots lifted half out of the water. Along their branches slunk wild cats and jaguars. But none harmed them.

For many days the Prince and the White Doe travelled together through this swamp, till at last, on a piece of sweet, fresh greensward, they came to a pavilion woven of leafy boughs. It had a graceful door of elmwood, and on the door was a delicately-fashioned knocker of lustrous, bright red cinnabar, shaped like a winged pear.

And the White Doe stopped before the door, and turned her head, and looked at the Prince imploringly.

So the Prince stepped up to the door, and lifted the knocker, and knocked three times. And the door opened, and there stood a beautiful maiden in a rose-coloured robe and a blue cloak over it. She wore a green girdle round her waist, and held to her breast she carried a green lyre with golden strings.

The beautiful maiden listened while the Prince told her his story, and did not say a word. Then the Prince said:

"It is in my mind that the White Doe led me to your pavilion that you might show me the way to the Princess."

But the beautiful maiden shook her head as she replied:

"No. I cannot show you the way to the Princess. Only the White Doe can do that. But lay your hand on the White Doe's heart. Can you not feel something amiss?"

The Prince laid his hand lightly on the White Doe's heart; and its beat beneath his fingers was so faint that it seemed to him no stronger than the fluttering of a moth's wings.

Then the beautiful maiden said:

"The White Doe led you to my pavilion because if her heart-beat grows yet fainter she will die, and then you cannot find your way at all to the Princess."

Then the Prince asked the beautiful maiden:

"What can I do to make the White Doe's heart-beat stronger?"

And the beautiful maiden replied:

"You can play to her on a magic lyre. Only the lyre's music must be no louder than a leaf's whisper far away; because otherwise her heart would burst for very rapture, and then you would have to give up your search for the Princess."

Then the Prince asked:

"What could such a magic lyre be strung with to make its music so soft?"

And the beautiful maiden replied:

"Only with the yellow floss of a silkworm's cocoon."

Then the Prince asked eagerly:

"Where can I learn to play such a magic lyre?"

And the beautiful maiden answered:

"I am a minstrel-maiden, and I know the secret. But it will take seven years to teach you."

Now the Prince thought such a secret was well worth seven years' study, so he stayed the seven years with the Minstrel-maiden, in the pavilion of leafy boughs. And the White Doe stayed with him.

And he learned everything that the Minstrel-maiden could teach him; and at last he was able to play a lyre strung with the yellow floss of a silkworm's cocoon, whose music was no louder than a leaf's whisper far away.

And the Prince was no older at the end of the seven years with the Minstrel-maiden than he had been at the beginning.

Then he said farewell to the Minstrel-maiden, and the Minstrel-maiden gave him a hazel-nut as a gift from her heart to his. And the Minstrel-maiden said:

"Keep it carefully, and do not crack it until you find yourself in grievous need of a minstrel's skill."

The Prince thanked the Minstrel-maiden, and put the hazel-nut away in his pouch with the Smith's monkey-nut and the Tailor's walnut. Then he set out from the pavilion of leafy boughs with the White Doe beside him. And protecting the picture of the Princess on her brow was the magic cover made of white nettles which was as clear and transparent as glass; and protecting her feet were the magic shoes of quicksilver which were as light as thistledown; and strengthening her heart was the music of the magic lyre strung with the yellow floss of a silkworm's cocoon, which the Prince held at his breast and played as they journeyed, and whose music was no louder than a leaf's whisper far away.

And the White Doe lifted her head and chose a path toward the west; and side by side, and with no one else with them, they followed it until they came forth from the swamp and saw before them a great water.

A little boat was moored to a leaning tree at the edge of the water, and the wood of which the boat was fashioned was so living that it had put forth roses. Two white swans were harnessed to the boat with golden ribbons; and when the Prince and the White Doe had stepped among the roses, the swans began to float away from the shore, drawing the flowering boat behind them. The water shone and sparkled and broke into stars and flashed forth little rainbows; and fishes of every brilliant colour swam up from the depths and accompanied the boat, with joyous fanning of their dainty fins and little airy leaps of happiness.

So for many days the Prince and the White Doe travelled over the water, till at last, in the far distance, they saw towers of shining crystal, roofed with gold.

And as they drew nearer the Prince saw that it was a palace, more beautiful than a palace in a dream, and that it was built in a countryside of fresh green fields and rich orchards and fragrant rose-gardens.

And in the haven below the palace there was anchored a glittering fleet of a hundred stately ships, with sails of many colours and with curiously-carved birds and beasts for figureheads.

The swans brought the flowering boat to the foot of a flight of white marble steps which came down to the edge of the water. And after the Prince had thanked the swans, he climbed the steps to a massive gate of beaten gold pierced into delicate lacework. And the White Doe went with him.

There was a golden knocker on the gate, shaped like the sun, with a magnificent ruby at its centre. And the Prince lifted the knocker and knocked three times.

And the golden gate opened, and a gate-keeper stood there in garments flashing with jewels; and when he saw the Prince and the White Doe he gave a shout of joy. And at that shout attendants came running; and their garments, too, flashed with jewels, so that their coming was like the flowing of rippling water in the sunlight. And they, too, shouted with joy at the sight of the Prince and the White Doe, and brought them with welcoming words and gestures into the palace.

And all along the shining crystal corridors ran the glad cry:

"The White Doe has returned, and with her the Prince who is to be the Princess's true love."

So they came into a crystal throne-room, with ceiling and pillars of gold. It seemed to the dazzled Prince to be ablaze with precious stones and brilliant colours and sumptuous cloths, for in it were gathered nine and ninety young and handsome Princes, all magnificently dressed.

And at the far end, on a dais, stood a golden throne; and on it sat a Princess in a robe of cloth-of-gold so thickly strewn with jewels that she seemed to the Prince to be clad in stars. She had flowing golden hair and a golden crown; and as soon as the Prince saw her he knew her for the Princess in the picture on the White Doe's brow. Only the Princess was far, far lovelier than her picture.

When the Princess saw the Prince and the White Doe enter the throne-room, she rose from her throne and descended the steps of the dais and came eagerly to meet them. And first she threw her arms about the White Doe's neck and bent and kissed her on both eyes. And then she turned and looked at the Prince.

In his plain, travel-stained green hunting tabard, the Prince looked painfully shabby among those other resplendent Princes. But the Princess did not seem to mind. She held out both her hands to him, and her face was as bright as the sun with her great joy as she said:

"Now do I know in truth that the Prince is come who is to be my true love."

At this a shout of anger burst from the nine and ninety Princes. And the face of the Princess lost its brightness, and she wrung her hands and said sadly to the Prince:

"Yet there are still three tasks to be performed. My father set them before he died, and only that Prince who can fulfil them may I marry. That is why these nine and ninety Princes are gathered here. And today is the day my father fixed for these tasks to be performed."

But the Prince was undismayed, and answered her cheerfully:

"If I am in truth the Prince who is to be your true love, then I and only I shall be able to perform the tasks your father set. Therefore rejoice with me that I am come in time, and explain to me the nature of the tasks."

Then the Princess grew glad again, and explained to the Prince:

"The three tasks are to rescue a little kingdom from Air and Fire and Water and bring it safe to Earth."

And the Prince asked:

"Where is the little kingdom?"

And the Princess replied:

"Outside the harbour there are a hundred ships all ready and waiting to sail in search of these adventures."

Then the Prince took his place among the other suitors with a stout heart. And the hundred princes left the palace of crystal and went down the steps of white marble to the harbour; and there each one chose that glittering ship whose coloured sails or carved figurehead pleased him best. And because the White Doe had led him to the Princess, the Prince who was to be her true love chose a ship which had a stag's head at its prow. And he said farewell to the Princess and went on board. And the White Doe went with him.

Then the glittering fleet of a hundred ships, with a hundred princes on board, set sail; and the Princess stood on the steps of white marble, and watched the ships grow smaller.

When they had been sailing for many days, they came to a part of the world where the sky was dark with vultures, who swooped upon the sails and tore them to shreds with their jagged beaks and claws. And they brought a whirlwind with them, so that the ships were driven about the sea and dashed against each other.

And the seamen on the Prince's ship ran to him, and fell on their knees, and begged that he would save them.

Then the Prince looked round at them all and asked:

"Who is there here who knows how to fight the vultures?"

And the seaman who knew most about such things, the one whose place it was to be in the crow's nest at the mast-head and keep a watch for land and storms and sea-serpents, replied:

"I have heard it said that if the sails can be mended and made all one piece again, the vultures will depart, taking the whirlwind with them."

Then the seamen all cried out together:

"Is there no tailor among us?"

And at that the Prince remembered the Tailor's walnut, which he was not to crack till he stood in grievous need of a tailor's skill. And he opened his pouch, and took out the walnut, and cracked it; and there inside it lay the tiniest, slenderest needle you ever saw, not an eighth of an inch long.

When they saw it, the seamen laughed the Prince to scorn, exclaiming:

"How can such a nail-paring of a needle save us from the vultures' whirlwind?"

But the White Doe bent her head, and breathed on the needle; and the Prince whispered over it:

"Little needle, little needle, help us with your tailor's skill!"

Then the needle began to grow and grow. And presently it stopped growing and replied:

"I will help you. But first I must be threaded with a pure sigh from a loving breast."

Then the White Doe sighed over the needle; and the sigh trembled through the needle's eye and flowed out into an endless thread, as thin as air and as strong as flax-fibre. And the needle flew up into the sails and began to weave in and out as swiftly as if it had wings. And presently all the tattered rags were drawn together, and the sails were whole and all of one piece again.

And immediately the vultures departed, taking the whirlwind with them.

Then the Prince's ship sailed on, and so did such other ships as had escaped the vultures and their whirlwind. And when the fleet drew together again, they found that three and thirty of the hundred ships had perished, and three and thirty of the princes with them.

For many days the seven and sixty ships which remained sailed on again together, until they came to a part of the world where the sea-bed was the home of grisly dragons, who thrashed upward through the water, breathing forth fire, so that holes were burned into the bottoms of the ships, and below deck all the ships were filled with flames.

And the seamen on the Prince's ship ran to him, and fell on their knees, and begged that he would save them.

Then the Prince looked round at them all and asked:

"Who is there here who knows how to fight the dragons?"

And the seaman who knew most about such things, the one whose place it was to keep the ship in good repair, replied:

"I have heard it said that if the holes in the bottom of the ship can be closed with iron doors, the dragons will depart and the flames will disappear."

Then the seamen all cried out together:

"Is there no smith among us?"

And at that the Prince remembered the Smith's monkey-nut, which he was not to crack till he stood in grievous need of a smith's skill. And he opened his pouch, and took out the monkey-nut, and cracked it; and there inside it lay the tiniest hammer and anvil you ever saw, not an eighth of an inch long.

When they saw them, the seamen laughed the Prince to scorn, exclaiming:

"How can such mustard-seeds of a hammer and anvil save us from the dragons' fire?"

But the White Doe bent her head, and breathed on the hammer and anvil; and the Prince whispered over them:

"Little hammer, little anvil, help us with your smith's skill!"

Then the hammer and the anvil began to grow and grow. And presently they stopped growing and replied:

"We will help you. But first we need for iron three pure drops of blood from a courageous heart."

Then the White Doe stood over the anvil, and on to it there fell three drops of blood from the picture on her brow. And under the clanging hammer the three drops of blood were forged into doors of red iron, as fragile as rose-leaves yet as strong as the hammer itself. And the doors of red iron lifted themselves from the anvil and closed the holes which the dragons' fire had burned in the bottom of the ship.

And immediately the dragons departed and the flames below deck disappeared.

Then the Prince's ship sailed on, and so did such other ships as had escaped the dragons and their fire. And when the fleet drew together again, they found that of the seven and sixty ships three and thirty had perished, and with them three and thirty of the princes.

For many days the four and thirty ships which remained sailed on again together, until they came to a part of the world where the water was enchanted into a dead stillness, so that they were utterly becalmed. The rowers bent at the oars until they were chafed and weary, but the ships did not move a hair's breadth.

The sea all about them was so stagnant that a scum grew over its surface, and on the scum crawled water-basilisks. And if their eyes rested on a man, the man was turned to stone. So, one by one, beneath the basilisks' stare, the rowers ceased rowing; and presently only stone men sat on the rowing benches.

The seamen on the upper deck of the Prince's ship, where the basilisks' eyes had not reached them, ran to him and fell on their knees and begged that he would save them.

Then the Prince looked round at them all and asked:

"Who is there here who knows how to fight the basilisks?"

And the seaman who knew most about such things, the one whose place it was to lead the song which the rowers sang to keep their oars dipping together, replied:

"I have heard it said that if the music of moving waters were played on the ship, the basilisks would depart and the men turned to stone would become living men again."

Then the seamen all cried out together:

"Is there no minstrel among us?"

And at that the Prince remembered the Minstrel-maiden's hazel-nut, which he was not to crack till he stood in grievous need of a minstrel's skill. And he opened his pouch, and took out the hazel-nut, and cracked it; and there inside it lay the tiniest lyre you ever saw, not an eighth of an inch long.

When they saw it, the seamen laughed the Prince to scorn, exclaiming:

"How can such a Tom Thumb of a lyre save us from the basilisks' stare?"

But the White Doe bent her head, and breathed on the lyre; and the Prince whispered over it:

"Little lyre, little lyre, help us with your minstrel's skill!"

Then the lyre began to grow and grow. And presently it stopped growing and replied:

"I will help you. But first I must be watered with pure tears from gentle eyes."

Then the White Doe bent again over the lyre, and slow tears fell from her eyes on to its strings. And the lyre began to breathe forth the music of moving waters.

And immediately the basilisks departed, and the stone men became living men and began to row, and the scum melted from the surface of the sea, and the ship began to sail.

But when the Prince looked round for such other ships as had escaped the basilisks and their stare, he found that of the four and thirty ships which had been becalmed the other three and thirty were becalmed still, their rowers still stone men.

So the Prince's ship sailed on alone.

And now the ship sailed straight back to the palace of crystal; and at the water's edge there burned a fire of charcoal in a golden brazier. And as the ship came into harbour, the Princess came down the steps of white marble as swiftly as a bird, her golden hair lying softly on her shoulders; and her face was so bright with joy and the jewelled gold of her garments flashed with such splendour that it seemed as if she swam in a flock of stars.

And she greeted the Prince kindly, saying:

"Welcome home, my true love; for now indeed have you proved that you are in truth that Prince."

But the Prince was astonished, and answered:

"How can that be? For I have not yet rescued the little kingdom from Air and Fire and Water and brought it safe to Earth."

Then the Princess laughed happily, and said:

"Oh, my true love, the little kingdom is this glittering ship, and you have rescued it from the vultures of the air and the dragons' fire and the water-basilisks, and brought it safe to land. So the tasks are all fulfilled."

Then the Prince rejoiced, and stepped ashore from the ship. And the White Doe came with him. Again the Princess threw her arms about the White Doe's neck and bent and kissed her on both eyes.

Then the Princess said:

"One last thing only remains. Take the magic cover of white nettles that is as clear and transparent as glass, and the shoes of quicksilver that are as light as thistle-down, and the lyre strung with the yellow floss of a silkworm's cocoon, and cast them all into the fire of charcoal in the golden brazier."

Then the Prince was very sad. For he remembered that it had taken him seven years to learn to make the cover of white nettles which was as clear and transparent as glass, and seven years to learn to forge the shoes of quicksilver that were as light as thistledown, and seven years to learn to play the lyre strung with the yellow floss of a silkworm's cocoon, whose music was no louder than a leaf's whisper far away.

And he remembered, too, that these things were very precious to him, because without their aid he would never have found the Princess.

But then he thought of his great love for her, and knew that he would do this thing because she asked it of him.

So the Prince took the cover of white nettles that was as clear and transparent as glass, and he cast it into the fire of charcoal in the golden brazier. And as it burned, the White Doe's head turned into the head of a Queen.

Then the Prince took the lyre strung with the yellow floss of a silkworm's cocoon, whose music was no louder than a leaf's whisper far away, and he cast it into the fire of charcoal in the golden brazier. And as it burned, the White Doe turned into a Queen down to the waist.

Then the Prince took the shoes of quicksilver that were as light as thistledown, and he cast them into the fire of charcoal in the golden brazier. And as they burned, the White Doe turned into a Queen from top to toe.

And the Queen wore a golden crown, and a red robe, and a rich purple cloak. And a heart-shaped clasp of gold, set with tiny perfect pearls and holding a picture of the Princess, fastened the cloak at her breast.

Then the Princess took the Prince's hand and laid it in the Queen's and said to him:

"This is my mother, who feared, when my father died, that the Prince who was to be my true love might not come to me in time. So, out of her great love for me, she became a white doe, in order to guide you to me and help you to fulfil the tasks my father set."

Then there were great rejoicings throughout the kingdom. And the Prince married the Princess; and the Queen and the Prince and the Princess lived happily together in the palace of crystal.

And as long as there are boys and girls who love this story, they will go on living there.

# The Kingdom of Beautiful Colours

Once upon a time there was a Kingdom of Beautiful Colours. In the middle of it stood a Cloud Mountain; and from the top of the Cloud Mountain you looked down on a wonderful rainbow, shining green and blue and yellow. The King had spent his whole life keeping that rainbow clean and fair. He went often to the top of the Cloud Mountain to make sure that the rainbow was still beautiful, for then he knew that all was well with the pastures and the forests and the cornfields of his kingdom.

Then time came for the King to go on a long journey; so he called his four sons to him, and he divided the Kingdom of Beautiful Colours into four parts, and he gave a part to each of his sons to take care of for him while he was away. And now from the top of the Cloud Mountain you could see four rainbows shining.

And the King said to his sons:

"My dear sons, I shall be away for three whole years. When I return, I shall go to the top of the Cloud Mountain. And if I see that you have kept your rainbows clean and fair, then you shall each keep the kingdom you have cared for and become its King. But if you have *not* kept your rainbow beautiful, then I shall have to take it away from you, and I am afraid that then you will have no kingdom at all."

Then the King bade his sons farewell, and set out on his long journey. And the four princes at once began to ask each other how best to keep their rainbows clean and fair.

The Eldest Prince suggested:

"Perhaps the wisest thing would be to ask our Fairy Godmother."

But the Youngest Prince reminded him:

"But you know she only leaves the Moon for one day in each year."

Then the Second Prince suggested:

"Couldn't we pay her a visit, as we used to do when we were small?"

But the Youngest Prince reminded him:

"But her silver ladders are so delicate, they probably wouldn't bear us now that we are bigger."

Then the Third Prince suggested:

"Couldn't we try them at full moon? They are much stronger then."

So at full moon the four princes went to the top of the Cloud Mountain, and climbed the silver ladders which rested on its summit. When they reached the Moon, they got into a silver boat and sailed along a misty river to the silver palace of their Fairy Godmother. There they found her, sitting beside a fire which she fed with mistletoe, stirring a great silver cauldron in which she was melting the Sun's gold to turn it into moonlight.

Then the Eldest Prince said to her:

"Dear Fairy Godmother, we have come to ask your advice."

And the Second Prince said:

"Our father has gone on a long journey, and he has given the Kingdom of Beautiful Colours to us to take care of for him while he is away."

And the Third Prince said:

"And if we keep our rainbows clean and fair, he will give us the kingdoms we have cared for for our own when he returns."

And the Youngest Prince said:

"So we wondered if you could tell us how to keep our rainbows beautiful?"

Then the Fairy Godmother ceased stirring the Sun's gold in the silver cauldron, and looked up, and smiled, and nodded, and said:

"Yes, my dear godsons, I can tell you. To keep your rainbows beautiful, you must keep your kingdoms happy."

Then the Eldest Prince asked her:

"Dear Fairy Godmother, how can we keep our Yellow Kingdoms happy?"

And the Fairy Godmother replied:

"By ploughing with devotion and sowing with joy and reaping with gratitude."

Then the Second Prince asked her:

"Dear Fairy Godmother, how can we keep our Green Kingdoms happy?"

And the Fairy Godmother replied:

"By letting only contented cows feed in their pastures."

Then the Third Prince asked her:

"Dear Fairy Godmother, how can we keep our Blue Kingdoms happy?"

And the Fairy Godmother replied:

"By planting a young tree for every old tree you cut down."

Then the Youngest Prince said:

"That sounds very, very easy! Is that really all?"

And the Fairy Godmother replied:

"The Sun's light holds sway in the bread:
Use it as the Sun would wish it to be used.
The Moon's tides hold sway in the milk:
Use it as the Moon would wish it to be used.
The Earth's might holds sway in the wood.
Use it as the Earth would wish it to be used."


Then the four princes thanked their Fairy God-mother, and sailed away from her silver palace in the silver boat, and came down the silver ladders to the Cloud Mountain, and from the Cloud Mountain to their father's castle.

And when they reached their father's castle, the Eldest Prince said to the others:

"Dear brothers, it would be difficult for us each to learn in only three years to be a good husbandman *and* a good herdsman *and* a good forester. Wouldn't it be wise for us each to learn to do one of these things well and to do it for us all?"

Then the Second Prince said:

"I will learn to be a herdsman and keep all our Green Kingdoms happy."

And the Third Prince said:

"I will learn to be a forester and keep all our Blue Kingdoms happy."

And the Eldest Prince said:

"Then I will learn to be a husbandman and keep all our Yellow Kingdoms happy."

But the Youngest Prince said:

"I will keep all my own kingdoms happy all by myself."

So the three eldest princes worked hard every day in their own and each other's kingdoms; and every evening they climbed the Cloud Mountain to make sure that they were keeping all three rainbows clean and fair.

But the Youngest Prince found that it was not as easy as he had thought for a prince suddenly to become herdsman and husbandman and forester all rolled into one, especially as it left him so little time for hunting. And one day, when he specially wanted to go hunting, and he knew that he ought really to be ploughing his cornfields ready for sowing the seed, he said aloud impatiently:

"How I wish someone would take this tiresome Yellow Kingdom off my hands!"

And no sooner had he said it than there was a zigzag lightning flash and a clap of thunder; and there beside him stood a black imp, with claws for fingers and a long black tail and eyes like coals of fire.

And the Black Imp said:

"I will gladly take your Yellow Kingdom off your hands."

"What do you ask in return?" said the Youngest Prince.

And the Black Imp replied:

"I do not ask anything."

"How good a husbandman are you?" asked the Youngest Prince.

And the Black Imp replied:

"I can make your cornfields yield fifty crops of corn where they now yield one."

"If you can do that, you are an excellent husbandman," said the Youngest Prince. "But you know that the Yellow Kingdom must be ploughed with devotion and sown with joy and reaped with gratitude? And that its bread must be used as the Sun would have it used?"

And the Black Imp replied:

"If I take your Yellow Kingdom off your hands, I must be free to plough and sow and reap and use its bread in my own way."

Now the Youngest Prince felt a little uneasy when he heard the Black Imp say this. But he wanted so badly to go hunting that he pushed his uneasiness aside and answered hastily:

"That is very reasonable. I agree."

And away he went to his hunting.

Then the Black Imp twirled his tail, and his eyes began to glow. And straight away the plough began to plough long zigzag furrows of itself, and the seed began to sow itself, and the corn sprang up in jerks, and grew and filled and ripened, and began to reap itself. And all the time the Black Imp just stood by with glowing eyes and twirled his tail.

So the first year went by. And at the end of the year the princes' Fairy Godmother left the Moon for one day to come down and visit the Earth. And as she alighted on the Cloud Mountain, she gave just one look at the four rainbows, then hastily spread her wings again and flew straight to the King's castle in search of the Youngest Prince.

She found him just returning from hunting; and she tapped him sternly on the breast with the silver crescent which tipped her magic wand, and demanded severely:

"What have you been doing to your Yellow Kingdom?"

"An excellent husbandman has taken it off my hands," replied the Youngest Prince with great self-satisfaction. "He is making it yield fifty crops of corn where it used to yield only one!"

"But that is terrible news!" cried the Fairy Godmother. "Your poor Yellow Kingdom must be as hungry as can be. No wonder it is unhappy!"

"Unhappy?" repeated the Youngest Prince. "Oh no, it wouldn't yield all this corn if it were unhappy. My Yellow Kingdom must be very happy indeed!"

"Do you really think so?" asked the Fairy Godmother. "Then come to the Cloud Mountain and see."

She touched him on the brow with the silver crescent which tipped her magic wand; and immediately they were both at the top of the Cloud Mountain. This was the first time for a whole year that the Youngest Prince had looked down from the Cloud Mountain at the Kingdom of Beautiful Colours. Now he looked at the four rainbows, and he saw that those of his three brothers were still clean and fair. But his own rainbow showed an ugly black stain where the yellow light had been.

Then the Fairy Godmother said sadly:

"Your Yellow Kingdom has been ploughed without devotion and sown without joy and reaped without gratitude. And now we will see if its bread has been used as the Sun would have it used."

She waved her magic wand, and a cloud enfolded them. And in the black cloud they saw a black imp with claws for fingers and a long black tail and eyes like coals of fire. And he was turning bread into yellow stones.

Then the Fairy Godmother waved her magic wand again, and a second cloud enfolded them. And in this cloud they saw many hungry little children crying out for bread.

Then a third cloud enfolded them, and before it the Fairy Godmother lowered her wand and bowed her head and crossed her hands on her breast. For a disc-shaped yellow radiance began to shine from the cloud, growing brighter and brighter till its brightness was more than the prince's eyes could bear. And out of the spreading yellow radiance there came a mighty voice, which said in golden trumpet tones:

"I am en-hungered. And ye feed me not."

And such an awe fell upon the Youngest Prince at the sight of that great radiance and the sound of that great voice that he threw himself down on his face. For he knew he was in the presence of the celestial Being of the Sun.

Then the cloud passed, and the Youngest Prince said earnestly to his Fairy Godmother:

"Dear Fairy Godmother, Couldn't you make my Yellow Kingdom happy for me again?"

But the Fairy Godmother replied:

"There is only one way to do that, and that is to find the yellow light which has been stolen, and to restore it to your rainbow. But only he who has taken away the light can give it back."

Then she touched the brow of the Youngest Prince with the silver crescent which tipped her magic wand, and immediately he found himself back in his father's castle. And there was the Black Imp awaiting him, with a huge, iron-bound chest.

Before the Black Imp could speak, the Youngest Prince turned on him angrily and said:

"My Yellow Kingdom is no longer happy, but has become an ugly black stain on my rainbow. You are not ploughing with devotion, nor sowing with joy, nor reaping with gratitude. Nor are you using its bread as the Sun would have it used."

And the Black Imp replied:

"But you agreed that I should be free to plough and sow and reap and use its bread in my own way."

The Youngest Prince remembered that this was so; but he said:

"I must take the Yellow Kingdom back and try to make it happy again before my father returns."

But the Black Imp replied:

"You cannot take it back. For you asked me to take it off your hands; and so mine it must remain till the King comes back to claim it."

Then the Youngest Prince asked anxiously:

"But how am I to face my father's anger when he sees the black stain on my rainbow?"

And the Black Imp answered:

"Do not fear. I have brought you something which will so dazzle his eyes that he will forget all about the black stain on the rainbow."

And he threw back the lid of the iron-bound chest; and the whole castle was filled with the blinding radiance of the precious yellow jewels which were heaped inside it.

"Where did you get all this wonderful topaz?" asked the Youngest Prince in astonishment.

"I made it out of bread," the Black Imp answered. "Take it — it is all for you. Put it into the Royal Treasury until the King returns."

The eyes of the Youngest Prince were so dazzled by the sparkling yellow jewels that he forgot all about the black stain on his rainbow. So he put the iron-bound chest into the Royal Treasury, and felt very pleased, and said: "Black Imp, you certainly are an excellent husband-man!"

"I am said to be quite a good herdsman, too," replied the Black Imp.

"Are you indeed?" said the Youngest Prince. "Just how good a herdsman are you?"

And the Black Imp replied:

"I can make your cows yield a hundred gallons of milk where they now yield one."

"If you can do that you are an excellent herdsman," said the Youngest Prince. "Perhaps you would like to take my Green Kingdom off my hands, so that I can go hawking."

And the Black Imp said:

"I would certainly like to take your Green Kingdom off your hands."

"What do you ask in return?" said the Youngest Prince.

And the Black Imp replied:

"I do not ask anything."

Then the Youngest Prince said:

"You know that only contented cows must feed in its pastures? And that their milk must be used as the Moon would have it used?"

And the Black Imp replied:

"If I take your Green Kingdom off your hands, I must be free to tend the cows and use their milk in my own way."

Now the Youngest Prince felt a little uneasy when he heard the Black Imp say this. But he wanted so badly to go hawking that he pushed his uneasiness aside and answered hastily:

"That is very reasonable. I agree."

And away he went to his hawking.

Then the Black Imp twirled his tail, and his eyes began to glow. And straight away invisible hands began to milk the cows in jerks, and the pails foamed high and jerked from under the cows of themselves, and other empty ones took their places and were filled and jerked themselves into the ever-moving procession of pails; and

never for an instant day or night, did the invisible hands cease milking. And all the time the Black Imp just stood by with glowing eyes and twirled his tail.

So the second year went by. And at the end of the year the princes' Fairy Godmother left the Moon for one day to come down and visit the Earth. And as she alighted on the Cloud Mountain, she gave just one look at the four rainbows, then hastily spread her wings again and flew straight to the King's castle in search of the Youngest Prince.

She found him just returning from hawking; and she tapped him sternly on the breast with the silver crescent which tipped her magic wand, and demanded severely:

"What have you been doing to your Green Kingdom?"

"An excellent herdsman has taken it off my hands," replied the Youngest Prince with great self-satisfaction. "He is making the cows yield a hundred gallons of milk where they used to yield only one!"

"But that is terrible news!" cried the Fairy Godmother. "How can the cows stay contented? Your poor Green Kingdom must be as thirsty as can be. No wonder it is unhappy!"

"Unhappy?" repeated the Youngest Prince. "Oh no, it wouldn't yield all this milk if it were unhappy. My Green Kingdom must be very happy indeed!"

"Do you really think so?" asked the Fairy Godmother. "Then come to the Cloud Mountain and see."

She touched him on the brow with the silver crescent which tipped her magic wand; and immediately they were both at the top of the Cloud Mountain. This was the first time for a whole year that the Youngest Prince had looked down from the Cloud Mountain at the Kingdom of Beautiful Colours. Now he looked at the four rainbows, and he saw that those of his three brothers were still clean and fair. But his own rainbow showed an ugly black stain where both the green light and the yellow light had been.

Then the Fairy Godmother said sadly:

"Contented cows no longer feed in your Green Kingdom's pastures. And now we will see if their milk has been used as the Moon would have it used."

She waved her magic wand, and a cloud enfolded them. And in the cloud they saw a black imp with claws for fingers and a long black tail and eyes like coals of fire. And he was turning milk into green stones.

The Fairy Godmother waved her magic wand again, and a second cloud enfolded them. And in this cloud they saw many starving babies crying for milk.

Then a third cloud enfolded them; and before it the Fairy Godmother lowered her wand and bowed her head and crossed her hands on her breast. For a chalice-shaped green radiance began to shine from the cloud, glowing brighter and brighter till its brightness was more than the Prince's eyes could bear. And out of the spreading green radiance there came a mighty voice, which said in silver trumpet tones:

"I thirst. And ye give me not to drink."

And such an awe fell on the Youngest Prince at the sight of that great radiance and the sound of that great voice that he threw himself down on his face. For he knew he was in the presence of the celestial Being of the Moon.

Then the cloud passed; and the Youngest Prince said earnestly to his Fairy Godmother:

"Dear Fairy Godmother, Couldn't you make my Green Kingdom happy for me again?"

But the Fairy Godmother replied:

"There is only one way to do that, and that is to find the green light which has been stolen, and to restore it to your rainbow. But only he who has taken away the light can give it back."

Then she touched the brow of the Youngest Prince with the silver crescent which tipped her magic wand, and immediately he found himself back in his father's castle. And there was the Black Imp awaiting him, with a huge, iron-bound chest.

Before the Black Imp could speak, the Youngest Prince turned on him angrily and said:

"My Green Kingdom is no longer happy, but has become an ugly black stain on my rainbow. Contented cows no longer feed in its pastures. And you are not using their milk as the Moon would have it used."

And the Black Imp replied:

"But you agreed that I should be free to tend the cows and use their milk in my own way."

The Youngest Prince remembered that this was so; but he said:

"I must take the Green Kingdom back and try to make it happy again before my father returns."

But the Black Imp replied:

"You cannot take it back. For you asked me to take it off your hands; and so mine it must remain till the King comes back to claim it."

Then the Youngest Prince asked anxiously:

"But how am I to face my father's anger when he sees the black stain on my rainbow?"

And the Black Imp answered:

"Do not fear. I have brought you something which will so dazzle his eyes that he will forget all about the black stain on the rainbow."

And he threw back the lid of the iron-bound chest;

and the whole castle was filled with the blinding radiance of the precious green jewels which were heaped inside it.

"Where did you get all these wonderful emeralds?" asked the Youngest Prince in astonishment.

"I made them out of milk," the Black Imp answered. "Take them — they are all for you. Put them into the Royal Treasury until the King returns."

The eyes of the Youngest Prince were so dazzled by the sparkling green jewels that he forgot all about the black stain on his rainbow. So he put the iron-bound chest into the Royal Treasury, and felt very pleased, and said:

"Black Imp, you certainly are an excellent herdsman!"

"I am said to be quite a good forester, too," replied the Black Imp.

"Are you indeed?" said the Youngest Prince. "Just how good a forester are you?"

And the Black Imp replied:

"I can make your forests yield a thousand trees where they now yield one."

"If you can do that, you are an excellent forester." said the Youngest Prince. "Perhaps you would like to take my Blue Kingdom off my hands, to give me time for feasting."

And the Black Imp said:

"I would certainly like to take your Blue Kingdom off your hands."

"What do you ask in return?" said the Youngest Prince.

And the Black Imp replied:

"I do not ask anything."

Then the Youngest Prince said:

"You know that you must plant a young tree for every

old one you cut down? And that their wood must be used as the Earth would have it used?"

And the Black Imp replied:

"If I take your Blue Kingdom off your hands, I must be free to fell the trees and use their wood in my own way."

Now the Youngest Prince felt a little uneasy when he heard the Black Imp say this. But he was impatient to start feasting, so he pushed his uneasiness aside and answered hastily:

"That is very reasonable. I agree."

And away he went to his feasting.

Then the Black Imp twirled his tail, and his eyes began to flow. And straight away axes without hands to wield them began to fell the trees, and the felled trees jerked away without timber-wagons to haul them; and the clearings in the forest grew wider and wider and wider, and still the axes without hands to wield them went on felling the trees, and all the time the Black Imp just stood by with glowing eyes and twirled his tail.

So the third year went by. And at the end of the year the princes' Fairy Godmother left the Moon for one day to come down and visit the Earth. And as she alighted on the Cloud Mountain, she gave just one look at the four rainbows, then hastily spread her wings again and flew straight to the King's castle in search of the Youngest Prince.

She found him just rising from feasting; and she tapped him sternly on the breast with the silver crescent which tipped her magic wand, and demanded severely:

"What have you been doing to your Blue Kingdom?"

"An excellent forester has taken it off my hands," replied the Youngest Prince with great self-satisfaction.

"He is making it yield a thousand trees where it used to yield only one!"

"But that is terrible news!" cried the Fairy Godmother. "Your poor Blue Kingdom will soon be quite denuded. No wonder it is unhappy!"

"Unhappy?" repeated the Youngest Prince. "Oh no, it wouldn't yield all these trees if it were unhappy. My Blue Kingdom must be very happy indeed!"

"Do you really think so?" asked the Fairy Godmother. "Then come to the Cloud Mountain and see."

She touched him on the brow with the silver crescent which tipped her magic wand; and immediately they were both at the top of the Cloud Mountain. This was the first time for a whole year that the Youngest Prince had looked down from the Cloud Mountain at the Kingdom of Beautiful Colours. Now he looked at the four rainbows, and he saw that those of his three brothers were still clean and fair. But his own rainbow showed an ugly black stain where the green light and the yellow light *and* the blue light had been.

Then the Fairy Godmother said sadly:

"A young tree has not been planted as each old tree was cut down. And now we will see if their wood has been used as the Earth would have it used."

She waved her magic wand, and a cloud enfolded them. And in the cloud they saw a black imp with claws for fingers and a long black tail and eyes like coals of fire. And he was turning wood into blue stones.

The Fairy Godmother waved her magic wand again; and a second cloud enfolded them. And in this cloud they saw many poor people perishing in the snow for want of wood for fire and shelter.

Then a third cloud enfolded them; and before it the Fairy Godmother lowered her wand and bowed her head and crossed her hands on her breast. For a square-shaped blue radiance began to shine from the cloud, growing brighter and brighter till its brightness was more than the Prince's eyes could bear. And out of the spreading blue radiance there came a mighty voice, which said in bronze trumpet tones:

"I am naked, and ye clothe me not; cold, and ye warm me not."

And such an awe fell on the Youngest Prince at the sight of that great radiance and the sound of that great voice that he threw himself down on his face. For he knew he was in the presence of the celestial Being of the Earth.

Then the cloud passed; and the Youngest Prince said earnestly to his Fairy Godmother:

"Dear Fairy Godmother, Couldn't you make my Blue Kingdom happy for me again?"

But the Fairy Godmother replied:

"There is only one way to do that, and that is find the blue light which has been stolen, and restore it to your rainbow. But only he who has taken away the light can give it back."

Then she touched the brow of the Youngest Prince with the silver crescent which tipped her magic wand, and immediately he found himself back in his father's castle. And there was the Black Imp awaiting him, with a huge, iron-bound chest.

Before the Black Imp could speak, the Youngest Prince turned on him angrily and said:

"My Blue Kingdom is no longer happy, but has become an ugly black stain on my rainbow. You have not planted a young tree for each old tree you have cut down. And you are not using their wood as the Earth would have it used."

And the Black Imp replied:

"But you agreed that I should be free to fell the trees and use their wood in my own way."

The Youngest Prince remembered that this was so; but he said: "I must take the Blue Kingdom back and try to make it happy again before my father returns."

But the Black Imp replied:

"You cannot take it back. For you asked me to take it off your hands; and so mine it must remain till the King comes back to claim it."

Then the Youngest Prince asked anxiously:

"But how am I to face my father's anger when he sees the black stain on my rainbow?"

And the Black Imp answered:

"Do not fear. I have brought you something which will so dazzle his eyes that he will forget all about the black stain on the rainbow."

And he threw back the lid of the iron-bound chest; and the whole castle was filled with the blinding radiance of the precious blue jewels which were heaped inside it.

"Where did you get all these wonderful sapphires?" asked the Youngest Prince in astonishment.

"I made them out of wood," the Black Imp answered. "Take them — they are all for you. Put them into the Royal Treasury until the King returns."

The eyes of the Youngest Prince were so dazzled by the sparkling blue jewels that he forgot all about the black stain on his rainbow. So he put the iron-bound chest into the Royal Treasury, and felt very pleased, and said:

"Black Imp, you certainly are an excellent forester! You are my best friend, and I would like you to be beside me when my father returns."

And the Black Imp gladly promised that he would.

And now the three years were over, and the King came back from his journey. The princes' Fairy Godmother had stayed down on Earth to welcome him; and as soon as he had greeted the four princes, she wafted him to the top of the Cloud Mountain, and he looked down at the Kingdom of Beautiful Colours. And he saw that the rainbow of the Eldest Prince still shone clean and fair; and so did the rainbow of the Second Prince; and so did the rainbow of the Third Prince. But the Youngest Prince's kingdom had no rainbow at all — only an ugly black stain where the rainbow had been. Then the Fairy Godmother wafted the King back to his castle, where his four sons were awaiting him. And the King said to them:

"My three eldest sons have kept their rainbows beautiful. But my youngest son's rainbow I cannot see at all."

Then the Youngest Prince clutched the Black Imp's claw to give him courage, and replied:

"But Father, you should see the jewels I have heaped up in the Royal Treasury!"

Then the King was angry and exclaimed:

"I did not tell you to heap up jewels; I told you to keep your rainbow clean and fair. And now it is so stained and black and ugly that I do not know whether it can ever be made beautiful again."

Then the Black Imp said quickly and ingratiatingly:

"Your Majesty, you are quite right; it is not worth your trying. It would be much better to let me take it off your hands for always."

"Perhaps it would," said the King. "Let me think for a moment."

Now the Fairy Godmother had listened very intently

when she heard the jewels mentioned; and, seeing that the King was inclined to let the Black Imp keep the spoilt kingdoms, she said to the Youngest Prince:

"I should like to see the jewels you have heaped up in the Royal Treasury."

The Youngest Prince was delighted to be asked to show the jewels, for he remembered that they had made him forget all about the black stain on his rainbow and that the Black Imp had said they would make his father do the same. So he led them into the Royal Treasury, and threw back the lids of the three iron-bound chests; and the whole castle was filled with the blinding radiance of the precious blue and green and yellow jewels which were heaped inside them.

Then the Fairy Godmother smiled happily, and said urgently to the King:

"Dear brother, do not give the spoilt kingdoms to the Black Imp to keep. For with these jewels the rainbow can be made beautiful again."

The Black Imp looked anxiously at the King to see what he would decide. And when the King decided to be guided by the Fairy Godmother's advice, the Black Imp began to gnash his teeth with temper, and his eyes began to glow and glow and glow; and in his rage he twirled his tail faster and faster and faster until he was whirling so fast himself that he launched himself into the air in a zigzag flash of lightning and disappeared in a clap of thunder. And nobody there ever set eyes on him again.

Then the King turned to the Fairy Godmother, and asked her:

"How can these jewels be used to make the rainbow beautiful again?"

And the Fairy Godmother replied:

"The light of the Yellow Kingdom is imprisoned in the topaz. The light of the Green Kingdom is imprisoned in the emeralds. The light of the Blue Kingdom is imprisoned in the sapphires. Once the light has been released, it can be put back into the rainbow."

"Who knows how to release the light?" asked the King.

And the Fairy Godmother told him:

"Only the Gnomes, for they are skilled workers with precious stones. We must ask the Gnome-Prince to help us."

She struck the floor of the Royal Treasury with the silver crescent which tipped her magic wand, and a cavern opened, and out of it came the Gnome-Prince, followed by his people. They were dressed in brown leather aprons, and had swarthy skins and long beards. They were no higher than the knees of ordinary people, and their heads were bigger than their bodies; and bigger than either was the hammer each one carried.

The Gnomes came into the Royal Treasury looking very sad and woe-begone. But as soon as they saw the blinding radiance and where it came from, they began to dance and sing and caper and to pick up the jewels in their strong brown hands and hug them to their hearts.

"Why are your people suddenly so happy?" the King asked of the Gnome-Prince.

And the Gnome-Prince replied:

"Your Majesty, when the cornfields and the pastures and the forests were unhappy, we were unhappy, too; for their roots are in our care. But now that he who took away their light has given it back, we can release it and restore it to the rainbow. Then the Kingdom of Beautiful Colours will be happy again; and we shall be happy with it."

"How long will this take?" asked the King.

And the Gnome-Prince answered:

"What the Black Imp took one year to do it will take us seven to undo: seven years to disenchant the topaz, and seven the emeralds, and seven the sapphire. In three times seven years the rainbow will be beautiful again."

Then the King gave the jewels into the keeping of the Gnome-Prince; and with great rejoicing the Gnomes dragged the three huge, iron-bound chests into their cavern, and the floor of the Royal Treasury closed over them.

Then the King turned to his three eldest sons and said:

"Because you have kept your rainbows clean and fair, you shall have your kingdoms for your own. But because my youngest son has now no rainbow, I am afraid he cannot have a kingdom, either."

Then the Youngest Prince felt very sad; and his three brothers were so sorry for him that they pleaded with the King on his behalf.

The Eldest Prince said:

"Father, remember that he was very young indeed when you went away."

And the Second Prince said:

"I am sure that now he would do better, Father, if he could try again."

And the Third Prince said:

"So won't you give him another chance?"

The King thought for a while. And then he said:

"Very well. The seven years that it takes the Gnomes to disenchant the topaz he shall spend with his eldest brother, learning to be a good husband-man. The seven years that it takes the Gnomes to disenchant the emeralds, he shall spent with his second brother, learning to be a good herdsman. The seven years that it takes the Gnomes to disenchant the sapphires he shall spend with his third brother, learning to be a good forester. And when he has learnt to be all three, he shall have his kingdom back."

Then the Youngest Prince made a solemn promise in his heart:

"The Sun's light holds sway in the bread:
I will use it as the Sun would wish it to be used.
The Moon's tides hold sway in the milk:
I will use it as the Moon would wish it to be used.
The Earth's might holds sway in the wood:
I will use it as the Earth would wish it to be used."

For he saw now that being a King meant much, much more than being able to hunt and hawk and feast; it meant spending one's whole life in keeping the kingdom's rainbow clean and fair. And as he resolved that this is what he would spend *his* life in doing, he heard the Gnomes in the cavern below begin gently hammering the jewels to release the rainbow's light.

# The Fisher-Prince with the Silver Apple

Once upon a time — when was it? When was it *not*? —
an old Fisherman lay dying in his hut on the shore of a
great sea. His young son watched beside him.

"My son," whispered the old Fisherman. "I am so poor
that I have nothing to leave you. But plant this seed on
my grave; and may it bring you fortune!"

And he gave the Fisher-Boy a shrivelled brown apple-
pip.

Then the old Fisherman died, and was buried. And
the Fisher-Boy planted the apple-pip on his grave.

The sun was setting when the Fisher-Boy came back
alone to the hut; so he took his net and cast it into the
sea, for he was hungry. When he drew it in, he found in
it a fish of pure gold, as shining as the sun. And the
Golden Fish cried out to him:

"Put me back into the sea, O Fisher-Boy!"

The Fisher-Boy thought that it would be a pity to eat
such a beautiful fish, so he put it back into the sea,
although he was so hungry. And the Golden Fish lifted
its head from the water, and said:

"Because you were merciful, O Fisher-Boy, you shall
be rewarded. Whenever you need wise counsel, come to
the sea at sunset, and call me, and I will come."

Then it sank and swam away.

And the Fisher-Boy went back to the hut, and had dry bread for supper.

The next day, when the Fisher-Boy went to his father's grave to lay a sea-poppy on it, he found that a tall stem had sprung from the shrivelled brown seed. The following day it had put forth leaves. And the third day it bore a silver apple that shimmered like moonlight on water.

The Fisher-Boy plucked the silver apple, and carried it carefully back to the hut, delighting in its beauty. It had a long brown stalk, and clinging to the stalk were two soft green leaves.

The Fisher-Boy wondered what to do with the silver apple. It was too beautiful to eat. He would have liked to bring it as a gift to somebody he loved, but now that his father was dead he was all alone in the world. So he thought he would ask the Golden Fish who had promised him wise counsel.

So at sunset he went to the edge of the sea, and called softly:

"Golden Fish! Golden Fish!"

The Golden Fish came swimming, and lifted its head from the water, and asked:

"What counsel do you need, O Fisher-Boy?"

Then the Fisher-Boy showed the silver apple to the Golden Fish, and asked what he should do with it.

"Toss it gently into the sea when the sun has set," the Golden Fish replied. "But remember to bring it back to land at sunrise."

Then it sank and swam away.

So the Fisher-Boy waited till the sun had quite set, then tossed the silver apple gently into the sea. And as soon as it touched the water, it began to grow and grow, until presently it had grown into a round silver boat, and the long brown stalk had grown into a mast, and the two soft green leaves had grown into two silken sails.

The Fisher-Boy stepped into the round silver boat and sailed away. All night long he sailed; and when dawn began to break, he found he had reached a country he had never seen before. He stepped ashore; and as the sun rose, the silver boat began to shrink and shrink, till presently it was again a silver apple with a long brown stalk and two soft green leaves.

In the distance the Fisher-Boy could see the red roofs and white towers of a city; so he walked along the shore toward it with the silver apple in his hand. On the way he passed a tall granite pillar, with a gold chain and a silver chain and a bronze chain hanging from it, and it puzzled him greatly why it should be standing there, quite solitary on the flat, deserted shore, right away from ships and dwellings.

When he came to the city and passed through the gate, he found the market-place filled with people. But they were not buying and selling, and shouting and jostling, and laughing and clapping each other on the shoulder, as people do in market-places. They were all clad in black, and they were all silent, standing quite still or else moving slowly and sadly, their eyes gazing sorrowfully at the ground.

Then one man looked up, and saw the Fisher-Boy. And a great shout of joy broke from him, so that others looked up too; and they also shouted, till the whole market-place was ringing. And they carried the Fisher-Boy rapturously toward the King's palace, crying aloud the glad news:

"The Prince with the Silver Apple has come at last!"

At the palace gates the Fisher-Boy was received with

the same glad welcome, and taken quickly along corridors of many-coloured marble, and ushered into the
throne room.

Inside the throne room it was very quiet. The only
sound was the sound of stifled weeping.

There were two thrones; and on one of them sat the
King, very magnificent in his crown and royal robes. But
he leaned his head wearily on his hand; and his face
was drawn with pain.

On the other throne sat the Queen, richly attired. But
tears were slowly falling from her closed eyes; and her
hand kept gently stroking the bright, unbound hair of a
maiden who knelt beside her. She wore a delicate robe
made of peach-blossom and a girdle of amethysts; and
her face was buried in the Queen's lap; and her
shoulders shook with sobs.

The King turned, sighing heavily, to see who had
entered the throne room. And when he saw the Fisher-
Boy, he stared in silence for a moment, as if it must all
be a dream. Then he started up, crying joyously:

"Weep no more, dearest daughter! For the Prince with
the Silver Apple has come at last!"

And he came down from the throne, and embraced the
Fisher-Boy, and drew him toward the Queen.

"Sire, I am no prince," the Fisher-Boy told him. "I am
only a poor Fisher-Boy."

But the King replied:

"Then a prince I now proclaim you; and you shall be
called the Fisher-Prince with the Silver Apple. Look up,
my daughter, and welcome your deliverer."

Then the Princess lifted a face as beautiful as the
morning. And she and the Queen dried each other's
tears, and welcomed the Fisher-Prince with the Silver
Apple warmly and with joy.

Then the Fisher-Prince with the Silver Apple said to the King:

"Sire, tell me the cause of your sorrow, and why you and the people speak of my coming in this way."

And the King answered:

"Once I had twelve daughters, all true and good and beautiful. Now I have but one, the youngest and best-beloved. For a fearsome dragon comes up out of the sea once in every year; and he would lay waste all my country if a king's daughter were not sacrificed to him. All my other daughters has he taken in turn; and now the day when my last one is to be taken is drawing near. Only the Prince with the Silver Apple can save her: this my wise men have told me. And now the Prince with the Silver Apple is come!"

The Fisher-Prince looked at the Princess and loved her. And he said to the King:

"Gladly would I give my life to save the Princess. But how should *I* fight such a dragon — I who all my life have only cast nets into the sea?"

"You must be armed," the King replied, "with a sword of heavenly iron. The heavenly iron you must find yourself. And the sword you must shape yourself."

"How can *I* shape such a sword?" asked the Fisher-Prince. "I who all my life have only cast nets into the sea?"

And the King made answer:

"The Heavenly Knight will teach you, in the Kingdom of the Stars."

Then the King had the Fisher-Prince with the Silver Apple arrayed as a prince should be arrayed. And he gave him strange and precious gifts — a golden dagger, and a drinking-cup made out of an opal, and a crystal thistle-flower, and the skull of an elfin horse.

And at sunset the Fisher-Prince with the Silver Apple went forth from the city and down to the edge of the sea, and called softly:

"Golden Fish! Golden Fish!"

The Golden Fish came swimming, and lifted its head from the water, and asked:

"What counsel do you need, O Fisher-Prince?"

Then the Fisher-Prince told the Golden Fish the story of the Princess, and asked where he might find the heavenly iron with which to make the sword to fight the dragon.

"You must sail in search of a shooting star," the Golden Fish told him. "But on your journey, remember, whatever helpless creature you may meet, be to it as merciful as you were to me."

Then it sank and swam away.

When the sun had quite set, the Fisher-Prince said farewell to the King and the Queen and the Princess, and gently tossed the silver apple into the sea. And again it grew into a round silver boat with green silken sails. And the Fisher-Prince stepped into the boat and sailed away.

Presently he came to an island. It was all one big, green meadow; and in the meadow a little blood-red calf was running to and fro; and it was weeping.

"Why do you weep, little calf?" the Fisher-Prince called out to it.

And the blood-red calf replied:

"They have taken away my mother. And now I am all alone in the world."

The Fisher-Prince was sorry for the little calf, so he said to it:

"Come with me, and I will take care of you."

So he took the blood-red calf into the silver boat; and

they sailed on until they came to another island. It was all one big, dense jungle; and at the edge of the jungle lay a fire-coloured lion-cub with its head on its outstretched paws; and it was weeping.

"Why do you weep, little lion-cub?" the Fisher-Prince called out to it.

And the lion-cub replied:

"My mother is trapped in a pit. And now I am all alone in the world."

The Fisher-Prince was sorry for the lion-cub, so he said to it:

"Come with me, and I will take care of you."

So he took the fire-coloured lion-cub into the silver boat; and they sailed on until they came to a tall rock towering out of the waves. And in an eagle's nest on the top of the tall rock a grey-feathered fledgling flapped its wings; and it was weeping.

"Why do you weep, little eagle?" the Fisher-Prince called out to it.

"My mother broke her wing, and fell into the sea. And now I am all alone in the world."

The Fisher-Prince was sorry for the fledgling, so he said to it:

"Come with me, and I will take care of you."

So he took the grey-feathered fledgling into the boat, and they sailed on until they came to where the sky was full of shooting stars, as thick as sparks flying from an anvil. And just as they came to land at day-break, one shooting star rushed past them, very close, and fell to earth with a great heat and glow and roaring.

As soon as the boat had turned back into an apple, the Fisher-Prince went in search of the shooting star. He expected to find it still a star, and still shining. But what he found was a deep crater in the earth, with the grass scorched at its edges, and at the bottom of the crater a hot, black, jagged, heavy stone.

The Fisher-Prince took the stone, and came back to his three companions. But now they were cub and calf and fledgling no longer as they had been when he left them. For while he had been away, in search of the shooting star, they had been growing, growing, growing, till now they were full-grown.

And now they no longer played pleasantly together, but were fighting one another.

The Fisher-Prince parted them, and calmed them, and made peace between them. And when the sun had set, the silver apple grew again to be a round boat on the water; and they all set sail once more.

And as soon as the shooting star was taken into the boat, it turned into clear white light; and it was no longer jagged, but shaped like a pointing hand. So the Fisher-Prince steered all night where its shining finger pointed; and at dawn they reached the Kingdom of the Stars.

A little distance from the shore they could see a bright fire burning. A sound of rhythmic clanging came from beside the fire; and with every clang there was a burst of shooting stars.

With his silver apple in one hand and his shooting star in the other, and with his blood-red bull and his fire-coloured lion and his grey-feathered eagle beside him, the Fisher-Prince made his way towards the fire. And as he drew nearer, he saw that it was a forge, and could see the Heavenly Knight tempering his great sword on the anvil.

The Heavenly Knight was clad in shining armour, with a cross and seven red roses on his breast. His frame was that of a hero; and his strength was that of a hero; but when he turned his head to greet the Fisher-Prince, his countenance was that of a young boy.

"What seek you with me, O Fisher-Prince?" he asked.

Then the Fisher-Prince told the Heavenly Knight the story of the Princess, and begged to be taught how to shape a sword with which he might fight the dragon.

"Have you found the heavenly iron?" the Heavenly Knight enquired.

The Fisher-Prince stepped forward to show him his shooting star. And as soon as the bull and the lion and the eagle no longer felt the Fisher-Prince's gaze upon them, commanding them to be at peace with one another, they fell to quarrelling again.

Then the Heavenly Knight sad sternly to the Fisher-Prince:

"I cannot teach you to shape a sword while you have such unruly companions. Come back to me when you have instead a golden eagle, a leaf-green bull, and a lion with a snow-white rose for heart, all brothers. Then will I gladly teach you."

So the Fisher-Prince went sadly back to the shore, and with him his three companions, no longer fighting, but very sorrowful because of the harm they had done him. And at sunset the Fisher-Prince went to the edge of the sea, and called softly:

"Golden Fish! Golden Fish!"

The Golden Fish came swimming, and lifted its head from the water, and asked:

"What counsel do you need, O Fisher-Prince?"

Then the Fisher-Prince told the Golden Fish what the Heavenly Knight had said, and asked how he could find the golden eagle, the leaf-green bull, and the lion with a snow-white rose for heart.

"First," the Golden Fish told him, "you must find the

Water of Life, the Sap of the Sun, and the Seed of the Dagger. But these you can only find with the help of those who have returned evil for your good and now would redeem the evil."

Then it sank and swam away.

Now the blood-red bull and the fire-coloured lion and the grey-feathered eagle were feeling repentant; and they came to the Fisher-Prince humbly, and begged him to let them help him.

"Are you willing, then," he asked them, "that I should send you away, and take as companions instead a golden eagle, a leaf-green bull, and a lion with a snow-white rose for heart, as the Heavenly Knight directed?"

And they all three answered, heavy of heart though they were at the thought of leaving him:

"If that is our only way to redeem the evil we have done you, we are willing."

Then the Fisher-Prince asked his three companions if they knew where to find the Water of Life.

"I know," replied the eagle. "You must travel across all the four Kingdoms of the Clouds. Beyond the fourth Kingdom is the Kingdom of Chaos. And the Kingdom of Chaos is filled with the Water of Life."

"How can I get there?" asked the Fisher-Prince.

And the eagle answered:

"I will take you there."

So the eagle took the Fisher-Prince between his great, strong, grey-feathered wings, and they began to soar in wide, ascending spirals, upward, ever upward through the high blue air, in mighty, sweeping curves.

Presently they came to the first Kingdom of the Clouds, a cold county where it was always twilight, so dark and heavy was its air with rain-mist.

Upward through this they flew to the second Kingdom

of the Clouds, a country long and low and flat, and full of glowing colours.

Still upward they flew through this to the third Kingdom of the Clouds, a warmer country of bright, white, airy mountain ranges.

And upward still through this they flew to the fourth Kingdom of the Clouds, where beautiful islands drifted like feathers in an ocean of warm light.

And so at last they came to the Kingdom of Chaos, a country so flaming with light that the Fisher-Prince was blinded by its radiance, though the eagle looked on it with steady eyes.

Everywhere, in streams and rivers and seas of dazzling fire, rang the Water of Life. And the Fisher-Prince took out of his bosom the drinking-cup made out of an opal which the King had given him, and he filled it with the radiant water.

Then the eagle bore him back, through the four Kingdoms of the Clouds, to where the fire-coloured lion and the blood-red bull awaited them.

Then the Fisher-Prince asked his three companions if they knew where to find the Seed of the Dagger.

"I know," replied the bull. "You must plough the earth where green grass is growing with the golden dagger which the King gave you. And wheat which sings and which shines like a candle will grow where you have ploughed. And when it has begun to sing and shine, you must pluck it. And that is the Seed of the Dagger."

"How shall I plough the earth with the golden dagger?" asked the Fisher-Prince.

And the bull replied:

"You must harness me to it with ropes of ivy and strands of honeysuckle, and we will plough together."

So the Fisher-Prince found a place where green grass

104

grew; and he took the golden dagger from his belt, and harnessed the bull to it with ropes of ivy and strands of honeysuckle. And they ploughed the earth together.

And wheat sprang up in the ploughed earth, and it began to sing and to shine like a candle. And the Fisher-Prince plucked the ears of singing, shining wheat. And he took from his scrip of purple leather the skull of the elfin horse which the King had given him. And in this he placed the wheat which was the Seed of the Dagger.

Then the Fisher-Prince asked his three companions if they knew where to find the Sap of the Sun.

"I know," replied the lion. "You must clear a space in the jungle, and purify it of all poisonous plants. And a vine will spring up there; and grapes will grow on the vine; and the grapes will begin to glow with a light like that of a ruby. And when they begin to glow, you must pluck them and crush them. And a juice like purple sunlight will flow from them. And that is the Sap of the Sun."

"How shall I purify the jungle of all poisonous plants?" asked the Fisher-Prince.

And the lion replied:

"I will show you when we get there."

Then the lion led the way to the jungle, which was a very rank and evil-smelling place. And they cleared a space in it.

Then the lion tore his own side with his claws, and took out his heart, and laid it on the ground. And immediately all the poisonous plants withered and died; and the evil stench disappeared; and in its stead a most sweet fragrance, like roses, filled the air.

And out of the lion's heart there sprang a vine; and grapes grew on the vine; and the grapes began to glow with a light like that of a ruby. And the Fisher-Prince plucked the growing grapes, and crushed them between his palms. And the Sap of the Sun flowed out like purple sunlight. And he took from the front of his red velvet cap the crystal thistle-flower which the King had given him, and in this he caught the flowing Sap of the Sun.

At sunset the Fisher-Prince went to the edge of the sea, and called softly:

"Golden Fish! Golden Fish!"

The Golden Fish came swimming, and lifted its head from the water, and asked:

"What counsel do you need, O Fisher-Prince?"

"I have found the Water of Life and the Sap of the Sun and the Seed of the Dagger," the Fisher-Prince told it. "What now must I do, O Golden Fish?"

And the Golden Fish replied:

"Give the Seed of the Dagger to the grey-feathered eagle. Give the Water of Life to the fire-coloured lion. Give the Sap of the Sun to the blood-red bull."

Then it sank and swam away.

So the Fisher-Prince took the skull of the elfin horse which held the Seed of the Dagger, and brought it to the eagle. And the eagle ate the Seed of the Dagger. And straight away his grey feathers turned to golden ones.

Then the Fisher-Prince took the drinking-cup made out of an opal which held the Water of Life, and brought it to the lion. And the lion drank the Water of Life. And straight away a snow-white rose grew where his heart had been.

Then the Fisher-Prince took the crystal thistle-flower which held the Sap of the Sun, and brought it to the bull. And the bull drank the Sap of the Sun. And straight away his blood-red hide turned to the living green of leaves.

Then the Fisher-Prince went back to the Heavenly

Knight, and with him went the golden eagle and the leaf-green bull and the lion with a snow-white rose for heart. And when the Heavenly Knight saw them, he rejoiced, and said:

"The eagle bought with his flight the Water of Life for the lion. The bull bought with his labour the Seed of the Dagger for the eagle. The lion bought with his sacrifice the Sap of the Sun for the bull. So have they served one another, becoming brothers; henceforth can they live together in peace. And now, O Fisher-Prince, can I teach you how to shape a sword of heavenly iron."

So the shooting star which the Fisher-Prince had found was heated at a forge and laid upon the anvil. And the Heavenly Knight taught the Fisher-Prince how to shape it into a keen sword, while the golden eagle and the leaf-green bull and the lion with a snow-white rose for heart looked on in great content. And presently the sword lay cold upon the anvil like a cross of light.

Then the Heavenly Knight buckled the sword in its belt about the waist of the Fisher-Prince, and bade him God-speed in his fight against the dragon. And the Fisher-Prince, having thanked him for his aid, came down to the sea with his three companions at the setting of the sun. And the silver apple became a boat as soon as it touched the water; and in it they sailed away from the Kingdom of the Stars.

And on the boat the sword of heavenly iron shone like a white flame, pointing the way to the country of the Princess.

At dawn they reached its shores, and walked at the water's edge toward the city. But when they drew near to the tall granite pillar which stood apart on the sands, they saw that a solitary figure drooped against it. And as they quickened their pace they saw that it was the

Princess, in her robe made of peach-blossom and her girdle of amethysts. And they saw that she was bound to the pillar with the chain of gold and the chain of silver and the chain of bronze.

Then the Fisher-Prince drew his sword swiftly, and tried to cleave the chains. But the Princess told him sadly:

"Nothing in the whole world can cleave these chains excepts the dragon's breath."

The Fisher-Prince looked to the left and to the right; but on all that deserted shore there was none to aid him in succouring the Princess. But the distant mountains and the red roofs and white towers of the city were thronged with people watching breathlessly from afar.

Then the Fisher-Prince heard a loud roaring behind him, like the sound of many waters. And, turning, he saw a gigantic wave approaching, churning and tossing the surface of the sea. And out of the wave rose a dragon fearsome beyond all his imagining.

Everywhere the dragon was armoured in overlapping metal scales. Three rows of cruel spikes ran along his back. He thrashed his enormous tail to and fro like a heavy, toothed whip. And from his cavern of a mouth came forth black smoke and orange flame.

The dragon came towards the Princess threateningly and triumphantly. And the Princess moaned, and shook her hair about her face to shut out the dreadful sight.

Then the Fisher-Prince rushed between them, and hurled himself upon the dragon with his sword held high.

Now began a long and weary combat. For the dragon was many times bigger and many times more powerful than the Fisher-Prince. And there was no chink to be

108

found between the closely overlapping metal scales where the sword of heavenly iron might penetrate.

The Fisher-Prince was scorched by the dragon's fiery breath, and scourged by his mighty tail, and bleeding in many places from his sharp and venomous talons. And presently he began to weaken from the burns and the beatings and the loss of blood.

Then he called out falteringly to his three companions:

"Help me, my companions, lest I fall and the Princess perish!"

Then the golden eagle beat with his powerful wings at the dragon's eyes, so that it could not see. And the leaf-green bull pinned down the lashing tail with his strong horns, so that it could no longer scourge the Fisher-Prince. And the lion laid his mighty paw on the dragon's heart, and held him prone upon the sand.

And as the dragon opened his mouth to breathe forth fiercer flame, the Fisher-Prince, with his last strength, thrust the sword of light deep into it. And the dragon lay spent and helpless, in a spreading pool of his own blood.

Then the Fisher-Prince would have killed the dragon; but the Princess called to him:

"Nay, do not kill him. For only by his breath can I be released from these three chains. But take my girdle of amethysts and put it about his neck and lead him by it; and he will be tamed."

So the Fisher-Prince took the girdle of amethysts from the Princess and put it about the dragon's neck, and held one end in his hand and led the dragon by it. And the dragon came quite meekly and quietly to the tall granite pillar, and breathed gently on the chain of gold and the chain of silver and the chain of bronze. And

109

they fell away beneath his breath, leaving the Princess free.

Then again the Fisher-Prince would have killed the dragon; but again the Princess restrained him.

"Nay," she said. "The dragon is to be conquered, but not killed. For it is his breath that warms the world. Men need the dragon's fire."

So the Fisher-Prince led the docile dragon toward the city by the Princess's girdle of amethysts. And the Princess rode upon the leaf-green bull. And the lion with a snow-white rose for heart paced beside the Princess, with her hand resting upon his fire-coloured mane. And the golden eagle perched in a friendly manner on the head of the dragon; and the dragon welcomed him.

And everyone in the city came streaming forth to meet them, clad in their gayest garments, singing and exulting and scattering flowers along their way. And at the gates of the palace the King and Queen met them in their crowns and royal robes, and fell on their necks and kissed them, weeping for very joy.

Then the Fisher-Prince with the Silver Apple was wedded to the Princess, and they lived in great content in the palace with the King and Queen. And the golden eagle and the leaf-green bull and the lion with a snow-white rose for heart ate from their plates and slept in their bed-chamber. And the dragon, with the Princess's girdle of amethysts about his neck, ranged the palace gardens, doing harm to none, but gently warming the world with the fire of his breath.

And if they have not died, they are all there yet.

# The Prince who had Two Eyes

Long, long ago, and far, far away, there was a country where the people had only one eye. Great, therefore, was the awe and excitement in the palace when a little prince was born who had two eyes.

The Queen at once sent a messenger to bear the tidings to the King, who was away in the forest, hunting; and as he passed out of the forest-gate of the city, the messenger met the King's Chief Counsellor, who was returning from the chase, attended by his Huntsman.

When the Chief Counsellor heard from the messenger of the birth of an heir to the throne, and one, moreover, who had two eyes and who would therefore be twice as clever as other people, he bit his lips with rage. For he had an evil heart and he coveted the Kingdom for his own.

It was just striking midnight as the Chief Counsellor and his Huntsman rode into the courtyard of the palace; and as the last chime died away they were dazzled and startled by sudden sweeping flashes of white light overhead.

They looked up, and beheld the night sky alive with mighty, scintillating Star-Beings. Right over the palace, bigger and brighter than all the rest, a majestic Star-Lion was striding across the heavens; and the sweeping of white light came from his shining wings as he spread them wide and began to fly down, in stately, awe-inspiring circles, to the earth.

And one by one, from this part of the sky and that, others of the brilliant Star-Beings spread their wings and followed him.

The Chief Counsellor and his Huntsman sat on their horses as still as if they had been turned to stone, watching the Star-Beings draw nearer and nearer till they reached the palace and disappeared through its walls. Then the chamber within was suddenly lit so brightly by the radiance of their wings that they could see a golden cradle, and the royal nurses seated near it.

But the nurses were sunk in a deep sleep, and no one but the Chief Counsellor and the Huntsman saw the Star-Beings enter.

The Star-Beings gathered about the golden cradle; and one by one they bent over the sleeping prince, and spoke a word of promise.

The first promised him beauty of form, and the second beauty of mind, and the third long life. The fourth promised him wisdom, and the fifth gentleness, and the sixth strength, and the seventh strange and high adventures. And the eighth said:

"Great hardships and great dangers are in store for him; but he shall win through them all."

Four still remained; and now these stepped forward with the gifts which they had brought down from the stars for their royal godson.

First came a mighty Centaur, with the noble head of a man and the body of a winged horse. In one of the baby's tiny hands he placed a golden bow, and in the other a golden arrow, saying:

"I endow him with the Bow of Striving and the Arrow

112

of Achievement. Ever shall the arrow return to the bow; and never shall the arrow miss any mark that is a right and meet one."

Next came the starry Crab, and said:

"He shall be the first mortal to wear the Cap of the Dark Star. With him shall the old order end and the new be ushered in."

And he drew on to the little prince's head a black cap with a crimson lining, closely fitting, with a point which curled over at the top.

Next came a shining, winged Maiden, carrying a spike of green corn, which she placed in the fold of the black cap, saying softly:

"I bestow on him the Food of the Blue Egg. He shall bring wonderful new harvests to his people."

And last came the Heavenly Lion, carrying in his mouth a red rose which had grown among the stars. He laid it in the prince's swaddling-clothes where they pleated over his breast, and said in ringing tones:

"I give to him the Everlasting Rose, and with it courage and a lion's heart."

Then, all helping, the Star-Beings covered the golden cradle with a cloak, wondrously wrought, of many shining colours.

And then a second time the Chief Counsellor and his Huntsman were dazzled by the flashing of their light-filled wings as they spread them, and flew upward, and entered again their mansions in the sky.

The heart of the Chief Counsellor had been black towards the child before; but it was blacker than ever now. For he knew that if the little prince lived long enough for all these starry blessings to bear fruit, then he himself could never come to be King. So he decided that the baby must be killed at once.

113

So he said to his Huntsman:

"Go quietly into the palace, and take heed that you do not waken the royal nurses. And take up the sleeping babe and carry him out through the desert-gate of the city. And in the desert kill him, and dip the cloak of many colours in his blood, then place it in the forest-gate, where the King will find it as he returns from hunting."

So the Huntsman silently stole into the palace, and wrapped the cloak of many shining colours about the sleeping child, and took him in his arms and bore him through the dark city to the desert-gate and so out into the desert.

The night was greying towards dawn as he laid the baby down on the ground while he took out his hunting-knife to kill him. But even as he did so he heard a savage growl, and looked up to see a fierce and hungry-looking lion looming angrily out of the misty twilight — so fierce and hungry-looking that he turned and fled from it in fear, and did not cease fleeing till he had reached the desert-gate.

The Chief Counsellor, when the Huntsman told him what had happened, felt sure that the wild beast would tear the little child to pieces; but he was angry with the Huntsman for not bringing back the cloak of many colours. So the Huntsman said:

"My lord, there is a house in the city where a child has lately died. He, too, had a star-cloak, which I could steal and dip in a lamb's blood, instead."

And the Chief Counsellor bade him do so.

So the Huntsman killed a lamb, and stole the dead child's star-cloak, and dipped it in the blood of the lamb, and laid it in the forest-gate. And as the King came swiftly home from his hunting, rejoicing in the tidings which the Queen's messenger had brought him, he saw the bloodstained star-cloak, and bade his attendants bring it to him.

And the King said:

"A wild forest-beast has stolen and devoured one of the children of the city. Send throughout the city and find the sorrowing parents, and bring them to the palace, that I may comfort them."

In the palace courtyard the King dismounted and came into the palace, very happy and eager to see the son who had been born to him. But the Chief Counsellor came to meet him wringing his hands with a woe-begone face, and told the King that a wild forest-beast had stolen the child while the nurses slept and carried him away.

Then the King held out the star-cloak; and the Chief Counsellor pretended to recognize it, and exclaimed:

"O King, that is the self-same cloak I saw the Star-Beings lay over the Prince at midnight. My Huntsman also saw it and will know it again."

And he sent for his Huntsman; and the Huntsman said it was so.

Then the King had all the forest searched; but nowhere was there any sign of the little prince.

Then the King, overcome with grief, went to his chamber, and shut himself in with his sorrow. And while he was there the attendants whom he had sent to search the city before he knew the prince had disappeared returned, bringing a woman of the city with them.

And they told the King:

"O King, we have searched all the city, and nowhere is there a child missing. But this woman of the city demanded to return with us to see the star-cloak, for the star-cloak of her dead child was stolen from her last night."

And as soon as the woman was shown the star-cloak, she cried:

"O King, it is the same!"

Then the King was perplexed, and bade the woman come with him, bearing the cloak, to the Royal Diviner. And they climbed the many stairs to where the Royal Diviner dwelt in a room of glass on the high, flat roof of the palace.

The Royal Diviner was very old — so old that no one knew *how* old — and very, very wise. He had long white hair and a long white beard; and his room was fragrant with magic herbs which he himself had gathered at the proper time of the moon, cutting them with a golden sickle and letting them fall on to a white cloth of fairest linen, so that they never touched the ground.

The King showed him the cloak, and asked:

"Is this my son's star-cloak?"

And the Royal Diviner looked at it, and said:

"O King, this is the star-cloak of a child of the city. The star-cloak of a King's son is far, far more lustrous and finely woven and delicate of colour."

Then the King asked the Royal Diviner:

"Is the cloak stained with a child's blood?"

And the Royal Diviner looked at it again, and said:

"O King, not so, but the blood of a lamb."

So the King gave the star-cloak to the woman who claimed it, and gave orders that she should receive rich gifts from the royal treasury. And then he turned again to the Royal Diviner, and asked, hoping again, and yet hardly daring to hope:

"Is it then possible that the little prince still lives?"

The Royal Diviner scattered magic herbs on the fire

which was burning in the middle of his room of glass in a brazier shaped like a five-pointed star; and a strong and sweetly smelling smoke rose from it and floated in curling vapours all about him. Then he brought forth his magic mirror, and stood very still and very long amid the curling vapours, gazing into the mirror until in it pictures grew before his eyes.

And at last he said:

"O King, the young prince lives. The mighty Lion of the Skies, under whose light he was born, protects him."

Then the King rejoiced, and urgently demanded:

"Tell me quickly where he is, that I may find him."

The Royal Diviner looked again into his mirror, then replied:

"O King, that is hidden from me, and will not be revealed until the time is ripe."

"Will he then be restored to me?" the King asked.

And the Royal Diviner, still gazing, answered:

"Not only so, O King, but your life shall be in danger and he shall save it."

"He will reign when I am gone?" the King asked further.

And the Royal Diviner gazed long into the magic mirror, and then answered:

"O King, he will, and that right nobly. For the Star-Beings have blessed him with precious gifts — the Bow of Striving and the Arrow of Achievement, the Food of the Blue Egg, the Cap of the Dark Star, and the Everlasting Rose. And he will use these gifts in the service of his people; and he will lead them on to their new destiny."

Then the King rejoiced once more and asked one last question:

"What does your magic mirror tell you of my son's two eyes?"

And the Royal Diviner gazed again, then answered:

"The young prince is the first-born of a race of two-eyed men, who shall be cleverer than the one-eyed men of our generation and who shall possess the earth. By the aid of the Food of the Blue Egg and the Cap of the Dark Star will they win their heritage."

Then the King was comforted, and went to tell the Queen and the Chief Counsellor. And the Queen rejoiced with the King; but the Chief Counsellor was dismayed, yet hid his dismay and pretended to share their joy.

Now the pictures which the Royal Diviner had seen in the magic mirror were true ones: the young prince *did* still live, and the mighty Lion of the Skies *was* protecting him. For when the Huntsman fled from the desert, in fear of the hungry lion, the lion had bounded forward to tear the little child in pieces. But just as the lion reached him, the young prince opened his eyes and looked at him.

Now this was the first human being with two eyes that the lion had seen; and there was something magic in the steady gaze of those two eyes in the pale light of daybreak which robbed the lion of his fierceness, and made him bow his head before the child, and murmur:

"Now do I know that I am in the presence of a King!"

He took up the baby gently in his mouth, and carried him carefully across the desert to his cave on the borders of the forest, where his hungry mate was awaiting his return, surrounded by their family of new-born cubs.

"So you have hunted down a man-cub," said the lioness, welcoming him. "Bring him to me quickly, O my mate, for I am hungry!"

"Yet I think you will not eat him," remarked the lion, laying the baby down in front of her.

The little prince opened his eyes and looked at her; and all her hungry fierceness went from her, as the lion's had gone from him; and like him she bowed her head before the child, and murmured:

"Now do I know that I am in the presence of a King!"

Then the lioness began gently to unwrap the cloak of many shining colours, till the baby lay before them in his white swaddling-clothes, with the golden bow and arrow in his hands, the black cap with the crimson lining on his head, the spike of green corn tucked into it, and the red rose on his breast.

And when the lion saw the rose, he recognized it, and exclaimed:

"Look — the rose of our Mighty Brother of the Skies! This little King is under his protection; and we must therefore give him ours. For the rose of the Heavenly Lion means that he will have a lion's heart."

"If he is to have a lion's heart, then must he drink lion's milk," laughed the lioness, very happy with her fosterling. "Come, little Lion-Heart!"

And she took the baby gently in her mouth and placed him among her sprawling new-born cubs, where he could drink lion's milk with them. And the little prince lay contentedly among them, and drank the lion's milk as greedily as they did.

So Prince Lion-Heart lived with his foster-parents in the cave on the borders of the desert and the forest, and repaid their care and protection with his love. And as he grew older, he hunted for them with his golden bow and arrow, so that they never went hungry. And never was there anything but love between them.

Now one day when Prince Lion-Heart was just

**119**

fourteen years old, the King and his court were hunting in the forest, and came very near to its confines, where it bordered on the desert. Prince Lion-Heart and the lion were lying hidden in a thicket, watching them ride by, when suddenly, with a mighty growl, the lion rose and hurled himself, raging, upon one of the riders.

The rest put spurs to their horses, and galloped away in fear. Only the King sat quietly on his steed beside the path, watching to see what would happen.

He saw a tall and handsome boy, with a strong and beautiful and well-made body, and with two clear and steady eyes beneath a noble brow, stride out of the undergrowth. On his head was a black cap with a crimson lining and a point which curled over at the top; over his shoulder he wore a cloak of many shining colours; and in his hands he carried a golden bow and arrow. A red rose burned over his heart; and in his cap he wore a green spike of some fruiting grass which the King had never seen before.

"Why do you strike down a man?" the boy demanded angrily of the lion. "Do you forget that I am a man, also?"

And the lion replied, standing with one paw firmly placed on the man he had struck down:

"Nay, Lion-Heart, I do not forget. Rather do I remember. For this is that wicked Huntsman who brought you to the desert and left you there to perish."

Then the King, marvelling, urged his horse a few paces forward, and called out, pretending to be very haughty and very angry:

"Boy, if this lion be your servant and has injured *my* servant, then upon *you* shall fall my wrath!"

Lion-Heart turned and looked at the King as the King had never been looked at before in all his life, for the boy stood quite firm and upright, his two clear eyes regarding the King steadily. Though he had never seen a King before, he recognized the golden crown about which the lion had often told him, and he knew he was in the presence of a King. This was the first time he had spoken with another human being, and his heart was beating fast at the encounter; but he answered the King's words quietly and proudly:

"O King, this lion is not my servant but my father."

The lion's heart swelled with love and pride when he heard the prince speak thus of him; but the King asked, perplexed:

"How can this be?"

The prince replied:

"My human father I never knew. But this lion rescued me from the desert as a new-born babe, and all my life he has cherished and protected me. Is he not then in very truth my father?"

The King was much moved and greatly astonished when he heard these words; and, turning to the Huntsman, he asked sternly:

"Did you bring a child to the desert and leave it to perish, as the lion says? Is this indeed truth?"

And the Huntsman, under the stern gaze of the King and the fierce gaze of the lion and the steady gaze of the boy, did not dare to lie, but answered, quaking:

"O King, it is truth."

Then the King asked again:

"Who bade you do so foul a deed?"

And the Huntsman answered:

"O King, my master."

Then the King was more astonished than ever, and asked:

"Why should my Chief Counsellor desire the death of a new-born babe?"

And the Huntsman answered:

"O King, the child stood in the path of his desires."

Then the King asked:

"How did the child do that?"

And the Huntsman answered:

"O King, the Chief Counsellor coveted the kingdom."

Then the King's pulse began to quicken as he asked:

"Who, then, was this child?"

And the Huntsman answered:

"O King, your son."

Then the King asked, with pulses beating quicker yet:

"Are there any signs whereby you would know the child again?"

And the Huntsman answered:

"O King, by the Star-Beings' gifts. By the delicate texture of the cloak of many shining colours; by the black cap with the crimson lining; by the golden bow and arrow; by the red rose grown in the gardens of the sky; and by the green spike of a fruiting grass unknown on earth."

Then the King remembered the Royal Diviner's prophecy that when the time was ripe the prince would be restored to him, and that with these very gifts he would lead his people to their new destiny. And warm love for the boy before him welled up in his heart.

And he was about to leap from his horse to embrace him when he saw the golden arrow speed past him from the prince's bow, just as a spear came hurtling from the thicket behind him and buried itself in his horse's flank.

Then from the thicket came a gasp of pain; and the lion went crashing past him, and appeared again, dragging out the body of the Chief Counsellor, with Prince Lion-Heart's golden arrow in his heart.

Now what had happened was this:

When all the court had fled at the lion's sudden leap upon the Huntsman, the Chief Counsellor had fled, too. But when he had galloped a little distance, he noticed that the King was not among them; so he drew rein, and looked back, and saw the little group — the lion mounting guard over the Huntsman, and the King talking to the forest-boy.

Even at a distance he recognized the Star-Beings' gifts, and so knew that the time had come which the Royal Diviner had prophesied, when the prince would be restored to his father.

So he dismounted from his horse, and crept quietly through the thicket, and hid behind a tree. For in his evil heart there was born a crafty plan — to kill the King, and then to kill the prince and the Huntsman; and to pretend that it was *they* who had killed the King, and that he had killed them in trying to save his royal master.

Then he would put the King's crown on himself, and blow the King's hunting-horn. And when the courtiers came riding back in answer to the summons, he would tell them that the King had bequeathed the kingdom to him, and had put his own crown on his head as a sign that he was to rule. And he knew that then all the court and all the people would accept him as their King.

He crept along so quietly that the King did not hear him; nor yet did the Huntsman even, for all his skill in woodcraft. But the prince and the lion, who had both lived all their lives between the forest and the desert, and who could even hear the grass grow and the flowers open, heard the faint sigh of the branches, and, looking toward the whispering sound, caught a tiny gleam which was the glint of the Chief Counsellor's spear as he aimed it at the King's heart.

Then, quick as thought, the prince had sped his golden arrow, spoiling the aim of the spear, so that it came to rest, not in the King's breast, but in his horse's flank.

When the King saw the Chief Counsellor with the golden arrow in his heart and saw how narrowly the spear had missed his own, he realized that part of the Royal Diviner's prophecy had already been fulfilled, and that the prince had saved his life. He leaped to the ground and embraced him, then blew a loud blast on his horn. And when the wondering courtiers came galloping back, he told them what had happened, and bade them rejoice with him because the long-lost prince was found.

Then the King would have caused the Huntsman to be killed; but Prince Lion-Heart begged that his life might be spared, and that he might take him into his own service. And when the King granted this, the Huntsman came and knelt before Prince Lion-Heart, and swore fealty to him, promising, if need arose, to give his life for him.

At the sound of the hunting-horn, the lioness and the prince's lion foster-brothers had come bounding to the thicket; and now the prince embraced them all, and said farewell, and promised not to forget them. And the old lion said:

"When the rose of our Star-Brother whispers, come back to the cave, and we will lend you our aid."

But one of the lions, the foster-brother who had loved the prince even more warmly than the rest, would not be parted from him, but cried:

"Withersoever you go, O my brother, be it to the city

or the desert or the unknown lands beyond, I will go, also."

And the prince, who loved him even beyond the others, begged that he might come with him; and the old King and the old lion gave their consent. So when Prince Lion-Heart, mounted on the dead Chief Counsellor's horse, rode away beside the King, the young lion ran beside him, with burnished mane upflung, in great majesty and gladness.

As soon as they reached the palace, the King took Lion-Heart to the Queen, who folded him in her arms and wept happy tears over him. Then he led him up the many stairs to the Royal Diviner's room of glass on the palace roof.

And as soon as he saw the prince, and noted his two clear steady eyes and the Star-Being's gifts and the exceeding fineness and delicacy of the cloak of many colours, the Royal Diviner said joyfully:

"O King, this is indeed your long-lost son, who shall lead his people to their new destiny. O King, issue a proclamation, bidding all the two-eyed youths and maidens come to the palace and swear fealty to him."

For another part of the Royal Diviner's prophecy had already been fulfilled — that the prince would be the first-born of a new race of two-eyed men. For after his birth, first one here and there, then more, and at last many babies were born throughout the kingdom who had two eyes instead of one.

But it was not necessary to issue any proclamation; for the news spread like wildfire through the city that the long-lost prince had returned, and that he was two-eyed and lion-hearted. And soon the courtyard of the palace was filled with two-eyed children, clamouring to see him. And Prince Lion-Heart came out to them, with his lion by his side; and gladly and eagerly they all swore fealty to him.

Then the old King would have given up his throne to Prince Lion-Heart, and set his own golden crown — the Crown of the Sun's Rays — upon his head. But the Everlasting Rose whispered to him that he must be King only of the two-eyed children, and grow up to manhood with them. And the Cap of the Dark Star whispered to him that he must wear itself instead of a crown.

And when the King consulted the Royal Diviner, to discover if it was good that Lion-Heart should break the custom of the kingdom in this way, the Diviner cast herbs upon his fire in the five-pointed brazier, and stood in the curling vapours, and gazed into his magic mirror; and presently he said:

"O King, the prince speaks truly. The Cap of the Dark Star must be his only crown until he has found the Blue Egg. And for the sake of his people it would be well if the Blue Egg were found before he comes of age."

Then Prince Lion-Heart asked where the Blue Egg was to be found. But though the Royal Diviner cast many magic herbs upon his fire, till the vapours curled in dense, intertwining forms, and though he gazed long and fixedly into his magic mirror, no pictures appeared in it in answer to the question.

Then the Royal Diviner shook his white head sadly, and sighed, and said:

"The old ways of wisdom are failing; and the day will come when the magic mirror will show no more pictures at all. For a time its pictures will still come to help and guide the King; but more and more, O Prince, must you find your help and guidance, not in the pictures of the magic mirror, but in the whispers of the Everlasting

Rose and the Cap of the Dark Star. To them must you turn now if you would find the Blue Egg."

So Prince Lion-Heart listened. And it seemed to him next morning, when he was wakened by the singing of the birds, that he heard this whisper from the Everlasting Rose:

"Seek the cave of your foster-parents."

So when the prince had dressed, he went to his lion foster-brother, and said:

"Today I go to the forest borders, to our father's cave."

And the lion answered:

"I will go with you."

So Prince Lion-Heart flung his star-cloak about him, and taking only the lion and the Huntsman with him, set off for the lion's cave. Great was the joy of the old lion and lioness at the sight of their two children. And the Huntsman, also, the old lion welcomed with kingly dignity; for when he had sworn fealty to the prince, all enmity had ceased between them.

But when Prince Lion-Heart asked where the Blue Egg was to be found, the old lion shook his magnificent head.

"I have heard tell of all the wonders of the forest," he said. "And I have heard tell of all the wonders of the desert. But never have I heard tell of the Blue Egg."

Then said the lioness:

"The forest is a great forest, and the desert is a great desert; yet are they both but small to the world which lies beyond them. But our blood-brother, the Wind, ranges that outer world, and there must be many tales of wonders blowing about its wide spaces whereof we have never heard. Were it not wise to ask of him?"

"You counsel well," approved the lion. And he told Prince Lion-Heart:

"The first Lion was blood-brother to both Wind and Fire. And blood-brothers are ever fain to serve each other."

So the lion went out into the forest; but the lioness said it would be better in the desert, where the Wind could not get entangled in the branches of the trees. And Prince Lion-Heart and the lioness and the young lion and the Huntsman all went with him.

And the lion lifted up his voice and called upon the Wind. And presently there was a great rushing sound, as of mighty wings. Then a soft voice from the air above them answered:

"I have come at your call, O Brother. What would you have of me?"

Then the lion said:

"O Wind, in all your travelling about the outer world, have you heard of the Blue Egg?"

The Wind was silent for a moment, thinking back over all the tales and wonders he had heard since the world began. Then again his soft voice spoke:

"O Lion, I have heard once only of the Blue Egg. The tale went that it hung by a golden thread from the leafless Tree of the Serpent, and that never could man possess it until a prince with two eyes and a lion's heart should go in search of it."

Then asked the lion:

"O Wind, where grows the leafless Tree of the Serpent?"

And the Wind made answer:

"That, O my brother, I know not."

Then the lion said to the Wind:

"O Wind, you who range the whole wide world on your rushing wings, could you not search for the leafless Tree of the Serpent?"

And the Wind replied:

"O Lion, though I can hear and speak, yet am I blind, and of myself I could never see it. There is only one way I could find it."

"What is that way?" asked the lion.

And the Wind replied:

"If I took the eye of a man up to the Air Throne of the Heavens."

Then the Huntsman cast himself at the feet of Prince Lion-Heart, and begged him:

"O Prince, let the Wind take my eye."

But the prince replied:

"Nay, O Huntsman. For you have but one, and if you give that, then are you blind. Rather let the Wind take one of mine, for then shall I still have one remaining."

But the Wind said:

"O Prince, only a prince with two eyes can be possessed of the Blue Egg; so if I took one of your eyes the Blue Egg could never be yours. Neither could I see the whole earth spread out below me with the eye of a two-eyed man, if I sat with it upon the Air Throne of the Heavens; but only with the eye of a man of the one-eyed race."

Then the Huntsman rose, and stood up very straight, and called loudly on the Wind to take his eye.

So the Wind took the eye of the Huntsman; and they saw it shining higher and higher in the air till it was like a large star, then like a small star. Then it could not be seen at all.

But in a twinkling of an eye there again appeared in the high blue sky a small star, which became a large star; and they heard the rushing sound of mighty wings, and a soft voice said above them:

"O Prince, from the Air Throne of the Heavens I have

looked with the Huntsman's eye over the whole earth, and I found the Blue Egg hanging by a golden thread from the leafless Tree of the Serpent, which grows from a skull on the top of the Ice Mountain."

"Where is the Ice Mountain?" asked Prince Lion-Heart.

And the Wind replied:

"It is in the far, cold North. To reach it you must cross first the desert, then the Tundra of Mosses, and lastly the Wastes of Snow."

Then the prince thanked the Wind and his lion foster-parents, and returned, with his lion foster-brother and the blind Huntsman, to the palace. And there he said to the King:

"Father, give me leave to go in search of the Blue Egg."

And the King replied:

"Go, my son, and may your search prosper."

And he would have sent the prince forth well attended with soldiers and servants. But the Cap of the Dark Star whispered to Prince Lion-Heart that he must go attended only by his lion foster-brother and the blind Huntsman.

So they three set out together, through the desert-gate of the city, and travelled toward the North.

Every day it grew colder, and the country grew more desolate, until at last they came out of the desert and into the Tundra of Mosses. And again every day it grew colder, and the country grew bleaker, until they came out of the Tundra of Mosses and into the Wastes of Snow. And still every day it grew colder, and the country grew more frozen, until, beyond the Wastes of Snow, they came to the Ice Mountain.

And high on the top of the Ice Mountain they could

see one solitary and leafless tree — the first tree they had seen since they left the desert-gate of the city. So they knew this must be the leafless Tree of the Serpent, from which the Blue Egg hung by a golden thread.

So they began to climb the Ice Mountain; and the higher they climbed, the colder did it grow. It was a frozen wilderness of cliffs and chasms. The Huntsman's hand was wound in the lion's mane, and the lion led and supported him. But Prince Lion-Heart struggled up crags and along precipices alone.

Sometimes clouds enveloped them in mist, so that nothing could be seen. Sometimes a snow-storm whipped and stung and blinded them. Sometimes the ice splintered beneath their feet, or broke away when they pulled themselves up by it to a higher ledge. But every time they rested, the prince could see more clearly the leafless tree on the top of the mountain, with a blue light, like that of a jewel, shining among its boughs.

At last they reached the summit, and found the tree growing out of a skull, as the Wind had said, and the Blue Egg hanging from it by a golden thread. And coiled about the slender trunk of the tree, and guarding the Blue Egg, was a green serpent.

"O Serpent," said Prince Lion-Heart, "I have come for the Blue Egg."

"You cannot take it, O Prince," replied the Serpent, "while I am coiled about the tree."

Then the Prince fitted his golden arrow to his golden bow, and aimed at the Serpent. But the Serpent said:

"It will not profit you to kill me, O Prince. For with my life would the Blue Egg vanish."

"What then must I do?" asked Prince Lion-Heart.

And the Serpent replied:

"You must uncoil me from the tree."

Then Prince Lion-Heart was starting forward to uncoil the Serpent, when his foster-brother the lion said warningly:

"Ponder well, O my brother, before you lay hands on the Serpent. Will you grasp it by the head or by the tail?"

Then Prince Lion-Heart paused and pondered.

And the Everlasting Rose whispered from his breast:

"To grasp it by the tail is the coward's way. Dangers should be faced bravely."

And the Cap of the Dark Star whispered from his head:

"To grasp it by the tail is the fool's way, also. For then can the head turn and rend you."

Then Prince Lion-Heart firmly grasped the Serpent by the head, and uncoiled it from the tree.

And immediately from the head of the serpent there sprang forth a white bird, who said to Lion-Heart:

"You did well, O Prince, to grasp the serpent by the head. Had you grasped it by the tail, a dragon would have come forth from it, who would have devoured you all."

Then Prince Lion-Heart would have taken the Blue Egg from the tree; but the white bird said:

"Before a man can possess the Blue Egg, he must bring life to this place of death."

"How may a man do that?" asked Prince Lion-Heart.

And the white bird answered:

"By bringing Fire to dwell here."

Then Prince Lion-Heart turned to his companions, and said:

"I have no knowledge of Fire. Think you that he would come at the bidding of a stranger?"

"Fire is my blood-brother," answered his foster-

brother the lion. "I will call him hither and beg your boon of him."

So the lion lifted up his noble head, and called with a loud voice upon Fire. And Fire came, bright, and warm, and glowing, and wrapped round with leaping flames. And at his coming, the prince and his companions grew less stiff and frozen, and the icicles on the Tree of the Blue Egg began to melt.

Then Fire shot forth a scarlet tongue of flame, and said:

"I have come at your call, O Brother. What would you have of me?"

Then the lion said:

"We have a boon to ask of you, O Fire."

And Fire replied:

"Say on, my brother."

"We would beg of you," said the lion, "to bring life into this place of death by dwelling here."

"Gladly would I bring life into this place of death," Fire answered. "But one thing is needful to enable me to do so."

"And what is that one thing, O Fire?" the lion asked.

And Fire replied:

"That a man and a lion should sacrifice themselves and dwell here, also. For only by abiding in a lion's strong heart and a man's red blood could I bring warmth into such coldness."

Then the Huntsman said:

"I will dwell here."

And the lion said:

"I will dwell with you."

And Fire said:

"Then I can also dwell here."

Then the white bird, with his beak, drew the golden

thread from the branch, and brought the Blue Egg to Prince Lion-Heart. And Prince Lion-Heart took it joyfully, and bade a sad and grateful farewell to his foster-brother the lion and the blind Huntsman, and began to clamber down the Ice Mountain alone.

And when he reached the valley below and looked up, the leafless Tree of the Serpent was covered with green foliage, and already the chill air was warming as if with summer's coming, and the ice was melting, and bright grass was springing, and singing birds were flying to and fro, where before all had been dreary, frozen desolation.

Then Prince Lion-Heart turned his face toward the South, and made his way across the Wastes of Snow. And the Wastes of Snow were blossoming. Then he made his way across the Tundra of Mosses. And the Tundra of Mosses was blossoming. Then he made his way across the desert. And the desert was blossoming, too. So at last he entered the city by the desert-gate, and was welcomed back with great rejoicing.

Now his twenty-first birthday was approaching; and in that country it was the custom, when the heir to the throne came of age, for him to become King. Then the old King, together with all his subjects who were aged, were arrayed in white raiment; and after a farewell banquet, they would go in a garlanded procession to a certain cave at the foot of the mountains outside the city.

One by one they would enter the cave; and in that kingdom they were never seen again. But it was said that the cave led under the sea and came out again in a far country where it was always summer, and where each King and his white-robed band were lovingly welcomed by all the Kings and subjects who had gone that way before them.

So on Prince Lion-Heart's birthday the city was hung with garlands, and all the old people were clothed in white raiment, and the youths and maidens in red. And Prince Lion-Heart, with his cloak of many shining colours over his rose-red garments, was led to the throne; and the old King took from his own head the golden Crown of the Sun's Rays, and would have set it on his son's.

But the Everlasting Rose whispered to Prince Lion-Heart:

"The golden thread of the Blue Egg is the new crown of this kingdom."

So Prince Lion-Heart gently took the Crown of the Sun's Rays, and set it on the old King's head again.

Then the Royal Diviner, standing beside the throne in his garlands and white raiment, said to the old King:

"O King, the prince does rightly. In the past all the Kings of this kingdom have been crowned with the Crown of the Sun's Rays. But today this people enters upon its new destiny."

So the Blue Egg was brought from the royal treasury, and they found that its golden thread fitted Prince Lion-Heart's head exactly; and the Blue Egg hung from it in the centre of his brow. And all the people saluted him with great love and joy, and called out in a voice of thunder:

"Hail to King Lion-Heart, who shall lead us into the future!"

When the feast was over, the Royal Diviner went to the roof of the palace, and burned all his magic herbs, and strewed ashes on the fire in the brazier shaped like a five-pointed star. Then he stoned his room of glass until it was quite demolished. Then he took his magic mirror, and said to the young King:

"The time has come which I have long foreseen, when pictures appear no more in the magic mirror. Henceforth, O King, you must be guided by the whispers of the Blue Egg and the Cap of the Dark Star and the Everlasting Rose."

Then the white-robed procession went, singing solemnly, through the mountain-gate of the city, with the King in his golden Crown of the Sun's Rays leading them, and next to him the Royal Diviner, bearing his magic mirror. And the youths and maidens in their rose-red raiment walked beside them.

They wound through the flowery plain to the cave at the foot of the mountains; and one by one they said farewell and entered it, still singing, till at length the last white garment fluttered and was gone, and the young King and his young subjects stood alone at the cave's mouth.

Still from within the cave came the sound of solemn singing, growing ever fainter, till presently the listeners could hear only silence. But even then the sweetness of the garlands which had been borne into the darkness still blew back to them.

Then the rose-red procession returned to the mountain-gate of the city. And the new King's reign began.

Now until Lion-Heart came to the throne, no one in that kingdom had ever worn cap or crown unless he was of royal blood. But now the Blue Egg whispered to the King that all who wished should be allowed to wear the Cap of the Dark Star which he had worn as prince. And all his subjects with two eyes rejoiced to do so.

And the Blue Egg whispered to King Lion-Heart, and King Lion-Heart explained to the people:

"In the days of our fathers, when men had only one

eye, there was one King ruling over many subjects; and only the King could wear the Crown of the Sun's Rays. But now the two-eyed race has entered on its new destiny; and in far, far days to come, it will build a wonderful new city out of precious stones. And in that city all men will be Kings and wear a new Crown of the Sun's Rays, which will grow from the golden thread of the Blue Egg."

Now the people of that Kingdom had always lived by hunting, and their Kings had always led them in the chase. And for a time, whenever King Lion-Heart led them, his golden arrow never missed its mark, and the city never lacked for food.

But one day the golden arrow wounded a lynx without killing her. And King Lion-Heart brought her back to the palace, and nursed her wound.

And the next day the golden arrow wounded a she-wolf without killing her. And King Lion-Heart brought her back to the palace, and nursed her wound.

And the next day the golden arrow wounded a bison without killing her. And King Lion-Heart brought her back to the palace, and nursed her wound.

And the lynx, when her wound was healed, stayed on in the palace, and grew gentle and affectionate, and loved to welcome King Lion-Heart on his return home and to lie before his fire. And when her kittens came, they were not wild at all.

And the she-wolf, when her wound was healed, stayed on in the palace, and grew clever and devoted, and loved to run beside King Lion-Heart whenever he went out riding, and to guard his cloak when he laid it aside to bathe. And when her puppies came, they were not wild at all.

And the bison, when her wound was healed, stayed on

in the palace, watching King Lion-Heart with dreamy, placid eyes while she ate unending grass. And when her calf was born, it was not wild at all, and shared its mother's rich, white milk with King Lion-Heart.

Then the Blue Egg whispered to King Lion-Heart:

"The lynx which dwells with man shall have a new name. What will you call it?"

And King Lion-Heart said:

"I will call it 'Cat.'"

Then the Blue Egg whispered again:

"The wolf which dwells with man shall have a new name. What will you call it?"

And King Lion-Heart said:

"I will call it 'Dog.'"

Then the Blue Egg whispered again:

"The bison which dwells with man shall have a new name. What will you call it?"

And King Lion-Heart said:

"I will call it 'Cow'"

Then the Everlasting Rose whispered to King Lion-Heart:

"The golden arrow refuses to slay these beasts any more, because they have become the younger brothers of man. Your people should no longer live by hunting; but let them cherish and nurture the beasts, and these will recompense them."

So the people began to give up the hunting ways of their one-eyed forefathers, and to keep cattle, who gave them milk and butter and cheese. And in time there was not one man in the city who did not have a cat to purr at his fireside and a dog to be his friend.

One morning, when King Lion-Heart was wakened by the singing of the birds, he heard the Blue Egg whisper:

139

"The time has come to sow the gift of the Heavenly Maiden."

And the Blue Egg told him how to plough the soil, and sow the seed of the fruiting grass till now unknown on earth, and how it would yield a thousand-fold, and how the grain should be made into bread, and the bread given to the people to eat. And this bread was to be the Food of the Blue Egg.

And with the eating of the bread it came to pass that every ninth night a new Blue Egg with a golden thread dropped from the King's Blue Egg, and he sent it through the city till he found one of his subjects whose head the golden thread fitted, and he gave it to him to wear.

So the years went by; and with each year, in this way and in that, King Lion-Heart led his people ever further into their new destiny. And at last the time came when everyone in his Kingdom wore the golden thread about his head and the Blue Egg on his brow.

Then the Everlasting Rose whispered to King Lion-Heart:

"When the Blue Egg lives upon every brow in the kingdom, the time has come for you to sail to the West in search of the talisman which will cause a new Crown of the Sun's Rays to grow from the golden thread."

So King Lion-Heart called all his people together, and told them of his quest, and that, long though he might be gone, yet would he come again. And together, a vast concourse, toward the setting of the sun, they passed out of the sea-gate of the city, and came down to the sea-shore.

The sunset made a wide red path along the water; and after he had blessed his people, King Lion-Heart stepped alone into his boat of ash-wood, the Blue Egg on his brow and the cloak of many shining colours laid over his white raiment. And he slowly sailed down the quivering, crimson way right into the heart of the sinking sun.

On the shore the people stood in silence, the Blue Egg flashing on each brow, while they watched the sun sink into the sea, taking King Lion-Heart with it.

Then, sadly but serenely, they returned by the sea-gate to the city and the morrow's duties; and in each heart was the sure knowledge:

"King Lion-Heart will find the talisman! King Lion-Heart will return!"

# The Quest for
# the Star of the Sea

*In the* Morte d'Arthur *and the* Mabinogion *and the* Chronicles of the Crusades, *stories a little like this story are told in language a little like this language.*

In the days of old there lived a young knight of princely blood, whose name was Sir Leonas. He was strong of body and stout of heart, but he was still untried as yet on the day when he rode forth from his father's court to seek adventure. Long and far had he ridden, and many fair wonders had he seen, when one day, at setting of the sun, he came forth from a forest to the verge of a grassy plain, and there beheld a tall green tower lifted against the sky.

As he pricked toward it, looking to find therein kindly harbourage for the night, he saw that a high wall of black basalt was built about the tower, and set in the wall were two great brazen gates, fast closed. He took up the brazen horn which hung beside them, and set it to his lips, and sounded it; but he heard no stir within the wall, and no porter came to the gates to open them.

But a gentle voice floated down from the air above him, saying:

"Who comes to the green tower?"

Sir Leonas looked up; and there, at a narrow lattice

set high in the green tower, stood the loveliest lady his eyes had ever beheld.

Her golden hair fell unbound over her robe of fair white samite; her face was pale and quiet; her hands were folded meekly on her breast. Her beauty scarce belonged to earth; and it grew as he gazed, moving the young knight strangely, so that eagerly and full courteously he told his name and lineage.

Whereat she said:

"Sore grieved am I, Sir Knight, that I cannot bid you enter and be refreshed with meat and minstrelsy. But the gates are fast; and there is none here save I alone; and I am a prisoner here within my bower."

Then red wrath fell on Sir Leonas that so lovely a lady should suffer such durance; and he cried:

"What evil sorcerer hath wrought you this great woe?"

But she, gravely smiling, answered:

"No evil sorcerer, but mine own step-mother. And though great woe hath she wrought me, yet of it shall come great weal, since through this it shall come to pass that none save only a true knight may ever win me."

Then asked Sir Leonas:

"How may that be?"

And she replied:

"The gates will open only to the touch of a talisman that is called the Star of the Sea. And only he who hath been proved true knight may find it."

"How shall a knight be proved true knight?" asked Sir Leonas.

And she made answer:

"He must fare forth into the world, doing so well as in him lies what task soever comes to him. And it may be that his time of testing will come and pass over him, and he not know it till he find the Star of the Sea there in his hand."

Then Sir Leonas made a vow that he would fare forth in quest of this talisman. And he spoke long with the maiden, he from below, standing upon the earth, she from above, 'twixt earth and heaven. And she told him her name was Biancabella, the white, the lovely one.

And that night Sir Leonas lay beneath the stars, in the shadow of the outer wall of high black basalt. And at the coming of red morning, he arose and blessed himself, and said farewell to the maiden, and rode away upon his quest.

Across three times three kingdoms he rode, through fen and forest, across white worlds and across green worlds; but nowhere did he find the Star of the Sea.

So he came at last to a stony shore; and there gat he down from his horse, and sat him upon a rock.

And a great weariness came upon him, so that he longed full sorely to leave this quest which had no ending, and to live only in fair dreams of his fair lady.

And out of the sickness and the fullness of his heart he began to spin a song:

> "Biancabella is so bright,
> Woven all of gold and white,
> She is fashioned of God's light.
>
> Gold the hair that floateth free.
> Pale and pure of face is she
> As the wind-anemone.
>
> Hands like lilies quietly fold
> O'er a heart of snow and gold —
> Hands that life and healing hold.

Ah, sweet lady, it were bliss
Might one but thy robe's hem kiss. . . .
But never shall I that, I wis."

And as he sat at his song-spinning, a cry of distress
rang out from the sea; and, looking seaward, he beheld
an aged fisherman, in a small boat that rocked
perilously as he strove with a net heavy beyond his
failing strength.

But the sight slipped from the young knight's mind
like water, so deeply sunk was he in his own dreams.

Then a second time the cry of distress rang out from
the sea. And this time Sir Leonas was stirred out of his
dreams for a moment's space, and thought:

"Pity it is there is none to aid him!"

But to aid him himself came not into his mind. For
knightly vows had he taken to rescue distressed
damsels and to rid kings of the monsters that devoured
their kingdoms; but to help fishermen draw in their nets
— such vows had he never made.

Then a third time the cry of distress rang out from
the sea. And this time Sir Leonas was roused out of his
dreaming, and a well of pity gushed forth in his heart,
so that he cried:

"Though I were the noblest king in Christendom, and
he my meanest serf, yet we are brothers!"

And he rose up from the rock whereon he sat, and
plunged into the waves, and came to the tossing boat,
and laid his strong young hands beside those ancient
weak ones. And so, with many pains and much labour,
together they drew the net to land.

Then said the aged fisherman to Sir Leonas:

"Lord, how shall so poor a serf as I do thankings to so
high a prince as thou?"

146

And Sir Leonas felt a great love and liking rising in his heart. And he, who had been bred delicately at the court of kings, and who sat ever at the high table on the dais, said now to this poor serf:

"Fair sir, I have ridden far today, and am a-hungered. Give me, I pray you, one of your fish, and your leave to sup with you."

And the aged fisherman said:

"Lord, gladly so will I do."

And he gathered wood from old shipwrecks, and built a fire on the shore, and broiled two of the fish thereon, and set one of the fish upon a round green leaf, and so brought it to Sir Leonas where he sat.

And when Sir Leonas opened the fish, to eat thereof, behold, a white light shone forth from a crystal which lay within the fish, five-pointed, like a star.

And when the aged fisherman saw it, he cried:

"Lord, surely Heaven hath done my thankings unto thee! For this is a right precious gem from beneath the sea; and what man soever shall find it, he shall prosper. Meet indeed is it that the net you drew to land should bring you the Star of the Sea!"

And when Sir Leonas heard that name, he rejoiced exceedingly; and, bidding a courteous farewell to the aged fisherman, he gat him to horse, and rode away swiftly. Nor did he cease riding till he came again to the green tower.

And there he took the brazen horn, and set it to his lips, and blew thereon three loud blasts. And then he touched with the precious gem the brazen gates, and cried aloud:

"Open to the Star of the Sea!"

And the brazen gates swung slowly open, with a noise

as of trumpets and tabors. And Sir Leonas rode through them like a conqueror.

Now beyond the brazen gates he found a courtyard, and beyond the courtyard rose the white wall of the inner keep; and set in the wall was a gate of silver, fast closed. And about the wall lay a moat, and a drawbridge over it.

So Sir Leonas rode across the drawbridge to the gate of silver, and touched it with the precious gem, and cried aloud:

"Open to the Star of the Sea!"

But the gate of silver stayed fast closed.

Then grey despair fell on Sir Leonas, that thus far he had achieved his quest, and yet no farther. And he groaned aloud, and would fain have cast himself upon the earth and beaten at the stones.

But a gentle voice floated down to him from the lattice in the tower, saying:

"Grieve not, Sir Knight. For right well hast thou wrought!"

But Sir Leonas answered:

"What boots it to win through the brazen gates, if the gate of silver bide fast closed?"

Then said Biancabella, the white, the lovely one:

"There is a Star of the Sea that can open this gate, likewise. But a knight, ere he may find it, must win through a further time of testing."

Then Sir Leonas made a vow that he would fare forth in quest of this second talisman. And again he spake long with the maiden, he from below, standing upon earth, she from above, 'twixt earth and heaven.

And that night Sir Leonas lay beneath the stars, in the shadow of the white wall of the inner keep. And at the coming of red morning, he arose and blessed himself, and said farewell to the maiden. And from the narrow lattice there fluttered down to him her sleeve of white samite, for him to wear upon his helm. And right joyfully so did he do.

So Sir Leonas rode away upon his second quest.

Across three times nine kingdoms he rode, over waste and moor and mountains, across white worlds and across green worlds; but nowhere did he find the Star of the Sea.

So he came at last to a forest so far-flung that it seemed to him it must surely stretch to the world's end. And as he journeyed therein, a great unrest came upon him, and he bethought him of all the pleasures of the court which he had put from him for this quest which had no ending. And he longed with a full sore longing that he might once more taste of them.

And, looking up, he saw before him a wondrous castle, wherefrom streamed lights and minstrelsy and the sounds of mirth and feasting. And without the gate stood two squires in rich array, who came forward courteously to salute him, saying:

"Noble Knight, the lord of this castle bids you to his feast. Sir, you are stained with riding; but within the castle await you scented waters, and the white hands of fair ladies to unarm you, and silken raiment and rich furs, and at the feast many rare dishes, and choice wines in jewelled cups."

Then fain was Sir Leonas to enter the wondrous castle. But when he made to dismount, his horse reared full suddenly, and bore him swiftly away along the forest path, until the castle was no longer to be seen and the uplifted voices of the squires no longer heard. And Sir Leonas scarce knew whether to beat his beast or bless it.

And as he rode on, in two minds about the matter, he heard voices raised in a jocund canon; and along a little path which ran athwart his own, a company of jongleurs went riding by full gaily.

And as they passed in front of him, they called full merrily to him, saying:

"Whither away, Sir Knight, with so sober a visage? Cast care away; and come with us, who know not care. For we make songs of the deeds which other men do; and right daintily do we fare; and right softly do we lie; for welcome are we in every castle in Christendom!"

Gladly hearkened Sir Leonas, and fain was he of fellowship so buxom and full of cheer. But when he made to turn into the little side-path to follow them, his steed stood as firm as if it had been rooted in the earth; and follow on foot he could not in his heavy armour.

So their gamesome carolling died away, and Sir Leonas abode alone on the forest path. And again he scarce knew whether to beat his beast or to bless him.

And as he rode on, in two minds about the matter, a cavalcade of ladies came to meet him, riding the other way along his path, richly bedight, and lovely beyond all telling.

They bore falcons on their wrists; and as they rode past, they cast bold, bright glances upon Sir Leonas, and said enticingly:

"Come hawking with us, Sir Knight; and right good sport will we show you."

Gladly hearkened Sir Leonas; and fain was he so to have done. But when he would have turned his horse about, it stood steady as a rock, fronting away from them.

Then said Sir Leonas to the ladies:

"Fain would I come with you, fair ladies; but it seems my horse hath another mind upon the matter."

Then said the ladies, laughing:

"Leave then your horse to take *his* way, and come you *ours*. Choose whichsoever you will among us all, and right blithely will she share her steed with you."

Then Sir Leonas dismounted, and would have gone to them. But his horse turned its head, and with bared teeth it took from the young Knight's helm Biancabella's sleeve of white samite, and cast it down before him.

And as Sir Leonas looked thereat, a vision arose before him of Biancabella, the white, the lovely one; and it seemed to him that from the sleeve of white samite there grew a fair white lily, with a heart of fair, pure gold within its snow.

And when he lifted his eyes to the ladies, he saw there growing snake-lilies, which are blotched and spotted like a serpent's skin and bear venom in their flowers.

And now these ladies seemed to him no longer lovely, but loathly.

So right gladly now did he remount his steed, and ride on, speedily, away from them.

So he came to a greensward in the forest, wherein stood an altar, full richly arrayed with a cloth of white silk; and there stood upon it a fair candle-stick, which bore seven great candles, all lighted. And the candle-stick was of silver. And beside the altar stood an old man, clothed all in white, full richly.

Then Sir Leonas came, and knelt upon the greensward. And his unrest fell from him, and he felt made strong for the doing of doughty deeds.

So he came to the hermit, and said:

"Good father, tell me where there may be dragons in this land, that I may forthwith slay them."

Then the old hermit looked long at him, and said:

"Nay, my son. Not for thee the slaying of dragons. 'Tis the lion *thou* must conquer. Follow this path; it will lead thee to where dwells a lion most fearsome, that spreads dread throughout this land. Go seek thou him; and God and my blessing go with thee."

So Sir Leonas rode forward, till he came to a part of the forest where great flowers fashioned and coloured like winged creeping-things hung from the trees about his path and breathed forth heavy odours. And as soon as the flowers touched his steed, it sank down beneath him in an enchanted sleep.

Then alone and on foot went forward the young knight.

And presently he heard the sound of a loud roaring, which made his footstep falter. And a great red beast with a mane of fire came toward him.

And when it perceived Sir Leonas, it crouched with swinging tail; then with a mighty spring it was upon him, and felled him to the earth, and there held him with its paw.

And when Sir Leonas felt its hot, rank breath upon him, his bones were turned to water and his flesh began to quake; till sudden the memory came to him that in him ran the blood of kings. Therewith opened he his eyes, and fixed them right royally upon the lion's. And behold, all its wrath departed, and it cringed before him, and laid its head upon his feet.

Then Sir Leonas arose and drew his sword, to slay it. And it made no movement to flee or to defend itself.

Then said Sir Leonas, marvelling:

"How shall a true knight slay a beast that awaits

death in this meek manner? I cannot deal the death stroke!"

And he set his sword again into its scabbard.

And when the lion saw this, it rose, and licked the young knight's gauntlet, and, taking it softly in its mouth, led him onward through the forest.

So they came presently to where the forest ended at the verge of a high cliff. And the lion led Sir Leonas by a winding path to the shore below.

There came they to a lake of clear water, wherefrom the lion, with his mouth, drew a flower, and brought it to Sir Leonas. And when Sir Leonas saw it, he marvelled much, for it was withered.

So, the lion leading, Sir Leonas left that shore, and climbed the cliff by the winding way, and came again into the forest. And when they reached the great flowers like winged creeping-things, his horse was standing, awakened from its enchanted sleep. And Sir Leonas mounted, and rode back to the hermit, the lion running alongside like a favourite hound.

And when the hermit saw Sir Leonas return with the lion making joyful fellowship with him, he was glad, and said:

"My son, well hast thou done in thy conquest of the lion. For it is better to subdue the lion than to slay it. It will yet do thankings unto thee in recompense."

"Already it hath so done," replied Sir Leonas, and showed the hermit the withered flower.

And when the hermit saw the withered flower, he was filled with joy, and said:

"Now truly art thou blest, my son. For this sea-anemone hath holy powers; and when a man layeth it on water, and it spreadeth its petals abroad, then shall his projects prosper. Meet indeed is it that the lion thou did'st spare should bring thee the Star of the Sea!"

And when Sir Leonas heard that name, he rejoiced exceedingly; and, bidding a courteous farewell to the hermit, he gat him to horse, and rode away swiftly. Nor did he cease riding till he came again to the green tower.

The brazen gates stood open; and in through them he rode, and across the drawbridge to the gate of silver.

And there he took the silver horn which hung beside it, and set it to his lips, and blew thereon three soft blasts. Then knelt he, and laid the withered flower on the surface of the moat; and lo, it unfolded into a fair white blossom, five-petalled, like a star. And therefrom came forth the sweetest savour that ever he had smelled.

Then Sir Leonas touched with the flower the gate of silver, and cried aloud:

"Open to the Star of the Sea!"

And the gate of silver swung slowly open, with a sound as of flutes and cymbals. And Sir Leonas rode through it like a conqueror.

Now beyond the gate of silver he found an inner bailey, and within the inner bailey rose the tall green tower itself. And at its foot was a little golden door, fast closed.

So Sir Leonas rode across the inner bailey to the little golden door, and touched it with the flower, and cried aloud:

"Open to the Star of the Sea!"

But the golden door remained fast closed.

Then grey despair fell on Sir Leonas, that thus far he had achieved his quest, and yet no farther. And he groaned aloud, and would fain have cast himself upon the earth and beaten at the stones.

But a gentle voice floated down to him from the lattice in the tower, saying:

"Grieve not, Sir Knight. For right well hast thou wrought!"

But Sir Leonas answered:

"What boots it to win through the brazen gates and through the gate of silver if the golden door bide fast closed?"

Then said Biancabella, the white, the lovely one:

"There is a Star of the Sea that can open this door, likewise. But a knight, ere he may find it, must cleanse his innermost heart."

Then Sir Leonas made a vow that he would fare forth in quest of this third talisman. And again he spake long with the maiden, he from below, standing upon the earth, she from above, 'twixt earth and heaven.

And that night Sir Leonas lay beneath the stars, in the shadow of the tall green tower itself.

And at the coming of red morning, he arose and blessed himself, and said farewell to the maiden. And from the narrow lattice she let fall a pearl, which she took from her own bosom.

"Guard it well," said she, "and use it freely. For therein are wondrous powers of health and healing."

And Sir Leonas received it joyfully, and laid it next his heart.

So Sir Leonas rode away on his third quest.

Across nine times nine kingdoms he rode, through wilderness wherein there dwelt no beast, and forests so black that no bird sang therein, across white worlds and across green worlds; but nowhere did he find the Star of the Sea.

155

So he came to a shore where the flowers and the sweet greensward were washed by the waves. And he heard a solemn song sung by many men's voices in time to the falling of oars on water; and he knew it for a song of the Crusaders. And he saw not far off in the sea a ship that sailed toward him, and on the deck stood many men, some in armour, some in pilgrims' weeds.

And Sir Leonas thought:

"This goodly company fares forth to cleanse the heart of Christendom. What better way to cleanse a knight's own heart?"

So he entered the ship, and mingled with the knights and pilgrims, and with them sailed to the Holy Land, and there went ashore, and so came to Jerusalem.

Now encompassing Jerusalem there lay so great an army, gathered from every Christian kingdom under heaven, that it seemed as if a second city of pavilions had been builded there. And here for many months sojourned Sir Leonas; and braver knight in all the army was there none.

For whether the Christians made an assault upon the city, or whether the Turks sallied forth and joined battle without the walls, ever was he in the forefront of the fight; and neither poisoned arrows nor Greek fire did he fear.

Oft-times his armour bristled with heathen javelins; and oft-times was he wounded sore and grievously; but the pearl from Biancabella's bosom healed every hurt.

And it came to pass that the Turks were so sore pressed that they prayed for a truce, and promised to deliver up the Holy Cross, and that all Christians should travel in safety to the Holy Sepulchre.

So the Christians made a truce for three years, and left Jerusalem, and, returning to the shore and there taking ship, set sail for their own lands.

And Sir Leonas sailed with them.

And after many day's sailing, a great storm arose, raging so furiously that the ships were driven hither and thither about the sea. Then rose many cries to heaven from the kneeling pilgrims. And Sir Leonas, above the sound of swirling waters, heard suddenly one prayer above the rest:

"Aid us, O Star of the Sea!"

And as Sir Leonas gazed upon the aged pilgrim who thus prayed, it seemed to him for a moment's space that he was the fisherman and the hermit in another guise.

And the wind changed, and the storm abated, and the waves were still. And all night the ship sailed by the light of the stars. And Sir Leonas lay on the deck beside the aged pilgrim, and made joyful fellowship with him. And about him, and within, was a great peace.

And that day dawned when the ship came again to the shore where the flowers and the sweet greensward were washed by the waves. And here Sir Leonas left the ship, bidding a courteous farewell to the pilgrim; and he took horse, and rode away swiftly.

Nor did he cease riding till he came again to the green tower.

The brazen gates stood open; and in through them he rode, and across the drawbridge to the gate of silver. The gate of silver stood open, and in through that rode he. And so he came to the golden door, with his hands empty but with his heart cleansed, and with no command, but with a prayer, upon his lips.

This time he blew no blast, nor used he outer talisman, but knelt without the golden door, and murmured:

"Aid me, O Star of the Sea!"

And the golden door swung slowly open, with no golden clangour, but in a silence full deep.

And Sir Leonas arose and blessed himself, and went softly through the golden door, and with bowed head climbed the winding stair to the maiden he most highly and most holily desired.